GLADLY,
HERE I COME

∽

JOY COWLEY

This book belongs to:

Mrs. Walde

The Wright Group®

Gladly, Here I Come

©Story by Joy Cowley
Cover illustration by Jim Hays
©1997 Wright Group Publishing, Inc.

The Wright Group
19201 120th Avenue NE
Bothell, WA 98011

Printed in the United States of America

10 9 8 7 6 5 4 3 2 1

ISBN: 0-7802-8306-6

For Lily, Lucy, Richard, Charlotte,
Timothy, Oscar, Phoebe, Max, and Edwin,
with love from their granny

CHAPTER ONE

The children figured that Joe was the worst actor in all of New Zealand. He came back from the phone, pretending it was no big deal, but his eyes were electric with excitement, and his mouth twitched into a grin so wide it made his voice squeak. His hands wouldn't stay still, either. When he had finished the story, he threw his hands out as though he were going to catch the world. "Anybody want another horse?"

Hannah sat so still that she could hear the blood pumping in her ears. Her father's words seemed to hang in large speech bubbles over the table, and she had to go over them again to be sure of their meaning.

Mikey was grinning around a mouthful of chocolate cake. Sky, extra noisy because it was his birthday, was banging fists on the table, rattling plates and knives, and bouncing cake crumbs. "Yeah, yeah, ziggy-bob, yeah! Get another horsie. Yeah, yeah, yeah!"

Sophie and Joe were looking at Hannah, who was still daring herself to believe it. Shadrach had a foal? She flicked through pictures in her mind: the horse trailer that took Shadrach away, and then his traveling companion, the beautiful chestnut thoroughbred Lacemaker. They had been left for a night in a paddock after the axle of the trailer broke.

Sophie was laughing. "Dear old Shadrach! Who would have thought it? A worn-out old draft horse and elegant Lacemaker, queen of the thoroughbreds."

"She falled in love with him!" shouted Sky.

Mikey said, "What are we going to call it? Shadmaker? Lacerach?"

Hannah's cheeks were burning, and her throat was thick with tears, which would start running if she spoke. Shadrach had a baby. Shadrach was dead, and yet he was still alive.

"The owner said the foal had to be killed," said Joe, "but Nigel smuggled it out in his van, wrapped in a blanket, and found another mother for it. He knew we'd be interested." Joe put his hands on the table and leaned toward Hannah. "I have a solemn question to ask you, Oh Hannah of the Wilderness. Do you hereby adopt this filly?"

Hannah let her breath out in a long, soft sound. "Gladly!" she replied.

"That's a good name for her," said Mikey.

Sky thumped the table again. "Gladly, Gladly, ziggy-bob, Gladly. We got another horsie. Gladly, Gladly."

Sophie came up behind Hannah's chair and put her arm around her. Hannah turned and let her eyes and nose run against the folds of her mother's denim skirt. Gently, Sophie stroked Hannah's hair and said, "Yes, it's a very nice name."

Chapter Two

A few weeks later, Gladly arrived on the farm. She was newly weaned, a fine chestnut filly with large hooves and a hairy, protruding lip. She had been handled by people since birth and was playful in human company. The first thing she did as she clattered out of the horse trailer was to bite Sophie on the seat of her jeans.

"They do that when they've been pampered," said Sophie. "You children are going to have to watch this one. She's full of mischief."

Gladly whinnied, ears pricked up, nose and mouth tasting the new air. She skittered sideways, tossed her head, and then circled the family, her neck stretched as she sniffed each of them in turn. Hannah put out her hand, and Gladly, looking for food, immediately nuzzled Hannah's palm. The filly's mouth was still small and soft, but the feel of it, the loose lower lip and sprouting hairs, made Hannah's heart beat like a rush of hooves. She looked into the filly's dark eyes, Shadrach's eyes, and saw her own reflection in them. A picture of Shadrach leaped out of her head and changed places with the filly, and she imagined Shadrach's laughing whinny echoing around the farm, from hills to sea. "Welcome home," she said to the filly.

At the end of the winter, when Gladly was ten months old, the family had an even bigger surprise—Eden McNab.

Eden was some kind of relative, so distant that Hannah had not known of his existence. He was introduced to them so suddenly it was as though someone had given birth to him fully dressed and named, ten years old and with a claim on their family.

They learned about him at a Friday night family conference. The whole idea of these conferences was that matters could be decided by everyone in the family, but sometimes Joe and Sophie were sneaky and had their own plans. As far as Hannah was concerned, the Eden McNab business was the biggest sneak since Shadrach was sent away to the dog food factory.

As always, the family conference was held at the table after the dishes were done. They all brought notes with things to be discussed. Mikey had some ideas for school lunches that he called "cordon bleu sandwiches." Hannah wanted a new halter for Gladly. The filly was leading well, and it was time the old rope halter was replaced with a new leather one. But before anyone could say the words "lunch" or "halter," Joe got what Hannah called his salesman smile and said, "Tonight we have something really big."

"Oh-oh," thought Hannah.

Joe glanced at Sophie, who said, "Joe and I want to tell you a story about a boy. He's the son of my cousin Stacey McNab."

Mikey frowned. "I didn't know you had a cousin named Stacey."

"Second cousin," said Sophie. "Her mother and my mother are first cousins. Stacey and I had the same grandparents. That would make you and Eden—let me see—third cousins."

"Who's Eden?" Mikey asked.

Sophie looked at Joe before replying. "He's about your age, Mikey. I'll tell it from the beginning. Eden didn't know his father. His mother brought him up until he was six, and pretty difficult it was for both of them. They moved around a lot, house to house, job to job. Then Stacey met this Australian man who wanted to marry her but didn't want the boy. Eden went to live with his grandmother while Stacey moved to Melbourne with her new husband. I suppose Eden was very unhappy. Anyway, his grandmother couldn't cope, and neither could anyone else in the family.

He ended up with Social Welfare and lived in a whole string of foster homes and group homes—seven to date. Imagine it! One strange place after another."

"It might be interesting," said Sky.

"Interesting?" cried Hannah. "It would be awful—just awful! What about his mother? She should take him. She shouldn't listen to her husband."

Sophie touched Hannah's hand across the table. "Stacey is dead. About a year ago she drowned in a boating accident."

Hannah closed her mouth. Her first thought was that it served her right. That would teach her for dumping her kid. Then, shocked by her callous reaction, she made herself feel sorry for the Stacey cousin. She conjured up a mental picture that was romantically beautiful: Stacey, cold and lifeless but with skin the color of pearls, her hair spread out like silk on the sea. But the trouble with pictures in the mind was that they never stayed still. Her imagination went on to produce sharks and blood. She shuddered and pushed her fingers against her eyes.

"Their canoe turned over in some rapids," said Sophie. "He got to the riverbank, but she didn't. The thing is, Eden now has no one. His grandmother isn't well. She couldn't take him even if she wanted to. His aunts won't try again."

"He's been officially labeled a 'child at risk,'" said Joe.

"What does that mean?" Hannah asked.

"In real terms, it means that the poor little kid has never had a chance, and unless something is done for him, his whole life is down the tubes."

"Why can't he come here?" asked Hannah.

"He can have the other bed in our room," Sky offered. "That's all right, isn't it, Mikey?"

Mikey shrugged. "Suppose so."

"I'll give him some of my toys," said Sky. "My battery car!"

"It doesn't work," Mikey said.

"It does if you push it."

"Not so fast!" laughed Joe. "We're not making any decisions yet."

Sophie unfolded a piece of paper. "You should know that Eden has problems. He is described as 'emotionally disturbed' and having a 'diminished sense of social responsibility.'"

"What does that mean?" asked Sky.

"He's a creep," said Mikey.

"No!" said Sophie. "Mikey, it means nothing of the kind."

"Just joking," he said.

Sophie gave him a long look and went back to the letter. "He's a compulsive nail biter. He wets the bed, and he doesn't do well in school.

At ten he has a reading age of seven. He has communication difficulties. As you can see, he has suffered a lot of damage, which is going to need time to repair."

Joe said, "Sophie and I reckon we've never yet met a child we couldn't get along with, but that's not the issue here. It's the effect he could have on the three of you. That could put stress on you and on us as a family."

"How bad is 'emotionally disturbed'?" asked Hannah. "What does he, you know, do?"

"I don't know," said Sophie.

"It's too soon for any decisions," said Joe. "There's a lot of love in this family, enough to help someone in need, I reckon. But for the moment, we're stopping with that thought. First, we have to meet him."

"How?" asked Mikey.

"He's in a group home in Christchurch. How would you feel about a trip next weekend? We could go to Christchurch on Saturday, do some shopping, stay overnight in a cabin at the campground, and come back Sunday."

Hannah said, "When would we see him?"

"Maybe he could stay the night with us in the cabin," Joe said.

"Wouldn't you have to get special permission?"

"They say it's all right," Sophie replied.

Hannah stared at her. "You've asked already?"

Sophie blinked and licked her upper lip. "We said we *might* come."

"If it's okay with you," Joe said quickly.

That was when Hannah thought to herself, "What a sneak!" They had it all arranged. Oh well, maybe she could try a sneak of her own. She smiled widely at her parents. "Great!" she said. "Gladly needs a new leather halter."

Chapter Three

Mikey told Hannah she should write a story about St. Georgina, who tried to rescue a prince from some dragons. He was being sarcastic, but she took it as a compliment and laughed. Moments later, she asked him to help her make some chocolate fudge for the poor little orphan boy.

Now they were in the back seat of the car, on their way to Christchurch. They were getting near Kaikoura, and the air was so cold that even with the old car's heat turned up, they needed a blanket over their knees. To their left, the sea was gray with medium-high waves breaking on a stony beach and leaving rolls of foam among the kelp and driftwood. On the right, the Kaikoura mountains rose so high that Mikey had to put his head down almost to Sky's knees to see their snow-covered tops.

Hannah was in her poetry mood about the snow. She raved on and on about its beauty, how pure it was, like white camellias, and please couldn't they stop for a while to admire it?

Mikey relaxed when Joe and Sophie pointed out that there wasn't time. He didn't mind Hannah raving on about the snow. It made a change from the poor little orphan theme. It was just that Hannah seemed to go overboard about some things. She never seemed to know that you went only so far and then there was a barrier called common sense. She sailed on right over it—over the top, you could say.

The whole family was a bit like that, with the exception of Mikey. Sometimes he felt he was the only person in control, and that made him uncomfortable. It was all right for Sky to rush into things. He wasn't seven yet, and little kids tended to be like that. But Hannah, at thirteen, was a terrible rusher, and Sophie and Joe, who were about as grown-up as they would ever be and practical in lots of ways, often got carried away by things. Enthusiasm was all right, but too much tended to make people blind. Mikey felt that he had been born to hold four sets of reins in his hands. He was always pulling back and saying things like, "Have you thought…" or "What about…" or "But just suppose…"

Sophie told him he was a worrier. Joe called him good old practical Mikey. They couldn't both be right. In fact, he knew they were both wrong. He didn't enjoy being responsible. Nor did he like them thinking he never got upset. It was just that someone had to stand back and think things through.

For days, the rest of the family had been suffering from Eden-itis, with Hannah the worst afflicted. She had wrapped the box of chocolate fudge in green tissue and had made a card to go with it. The card contained a long poem about warm friendship banishing bitter winds and cold fate. Mikey told her to burn it.

"What's wrong with it?"

"It's pukifying! That's what's wrong."

Her eyes had filled with tears, and he had felt awful for upsetting her. Hannah was truly a remarkable person. He always thought that she was like some unique designer car, made with more gadgets and more power than could ever be used. Everything about her was beautiful and magic and surprising and special—and exaggerated. Mikey admired Hannah more than anyone he knew, but at the same time he found her exhausting. He was glad that sisters and brothers weren't required by law to live in the same house for the rest of their lives.

"It's not pukifying!" she said. "It's the truth!"

"What truth, Han? You haven't even met him. That's stuff you've just made up. Come on, get real!"

That was when she told him he was jealous.

Mikey had no complaints about the hours spent shopping in Christchurch. That was cool fun. Literally. The city was like one huge freezer, even though it was early spring, but the stores were warm and full of interesting things. Hannah got the halter she wanted for Gladly, Sophie bought some massage oils at a health food shop, and then they all went to see the model railroad exhibition.

Mikey thought the exhibition would have made any trip worthwhile. There was a room bigger than their Waitaria Bay school, and it was filled with layouts of all sizes. His favorite was a huge display spread like a Swiss mountain scene with funicular railways and cable cars high up, and long passenger and freight trains snaking in and out of tunnels and valleys. The details were perfect. Lights came on and signals dropped as the trains slid into miniature stations filled with people. The cable car, swinging up the mountainside on copper wire, also had people in it, with tiny faces pressed against the glass. Miniature pine forests at the foot of the mountains turned to scrub, then to moss and rocks, and finally to snow. In the valleys, people cut firewood and pushed milk carts outside houses that had red flowers in window boxes. Cows had bells hung around their necks. A waterwheel turned in a miniature stream.

There was even a bulldozer doing some road work, its blade lifting up and down.

Sky was shrieking, "Look! Look!" while jumping up and down and holding the seat of his pants the way he did when he was so excited that he didn't know what else to do. Mikey smiled. He was also excited, but in a different way. He was feeling a great squeeze of love in his chest. He had to have a train set like this—and he would, he would! If it took him all his life, he'd get it. He'd start now. He'd save his allowance for the basic tracks and one engine, one perfect little steam engine with solid wheels and polished pistons. Definitely! And when he was a famous chef cooking in the best restaurants for thousands of dollars, he'd be able to build...

"Mikey?" Hannah was beside him. "We should have brought Eden to this. He would have loved it."

"How do you know?" he said. "He might really hate trains."

She stared at him.

"Not everyone likes models," Mikey said, trying to ease the hurt in her eyes. "Some people think they're pointless."

"Pukifying?" she said.

He shrugged. What was the use of talking?

Hannah moved on to Sophie and Joe. "Why didn't we bring Eden to this? Wouldn't they let him out?"

Sophie said, "Hannah dear, it's not a matter of anyone being let out. We did ask, but the train exhibition's been here a long time, and the children from the home saw it a couple of weeks ago. I suppose he could have seen it again. We didn't consider that."

Mikey glanced at Hannah and saw the bruised look. "Yeah," he said quickly. "You could see it over and over and not get sick of it."

They stayed until after four and then went out into the darkening street, where the wind rattled signs and shivered daffodils in planter boxes. Mikey felt that a shade had been pulled down in front of his eyes. Everywhere he looked, trains rushed over his vision like ghosts. He must talk to Sophie and Joe about it. A simple figure-eight track would be best to start with.

Sophie drove to the campground, dropped them off outside their cabin, and then went to pick up Eden from the children's home. "Be back in half an hour," she said.

Joe unlocked the cabin door, and they took the boxes of supplies and sleeping bags into a room set up for six people. There were three sets of bunks with mattresses and pillows at one end, and a small kitchen at the other. Between the bed and kitchen areas was a table with six chairs. The bathroom door was behind it.

While Hannah and Joe unrolled the sleeping bags, including the one they had brought for Eden, Mikey put pillow cases on all the pillows, and Sky jumped from one top bunk to another. There was a small wall heater that worked with coins in a slot, and within minutes the cabin was as warm as a sauna. When everything was unpacked, Mikey got out some playing cards, and they sat down to a game of 500.

Sky was yahooing about winning the first game when they heard car wheels crunching on the gravel outside. The cards slammed down on the table, and Joe, Mikey, and Sky collided with each other to get to the door. Only Hannah stayed seated.

Joe was outside making welcoming noises. The car doors closed, one after the other, and Sophie and Eden came in.

"This is Eden," Sophie announced.

"Hello," Mikey said.

He thought, "Well, Hannah's 'poor little orphan kid' is about half right." The kid was little, about the same height as Sky, and on the skinny side. But he didn't look poor. He had on cool gear—new sneakers, a leather jacket with zippers everywhere, a really flashy watch, and a diamond earring in his left ear. He didn't resemble anyone they knew in Sophie's family. He had fair hair, curly, and a V-shaped face, wide at the top and narrow at the chin, with sticking-out ears and slanting eyes. As faces went, it was unusual but nice looking, like the face of a kitten. The kid looked at Mikey, gave a half-smile, and looked away again.

Sophie said, "That's Mikey, and over here is Hannah—"

Sky pushed in. "I'm Sky, and before you ask, it's S-K-Y. Sometimes I get bored and change it. You ever change your name?"

"Sky is six and a half, and Hannah is thirteen," said Sophie. "I think Hannah might have a present for you."

Hannah passed the box of fudge to Eden. "I'm very glad to meet you—cousin," she said in a small, breathless voice.

Eden took the package, gave Hannah another of his half-smiles, and stood there as though he was waiting for someone to wind up a key in his back and get him moving.

"Where do you want to sleep, Eden?" asked Joe. "Choose any bunk you like."

Eden looked at the floor and shrugged.

"It's chocolate fudge with walnuts," said Hannah in a slightly more normal voice. "Mikey and I made it."

He glanced at the package in his hand.

"I hope you like walnuts. They came off our own trees."

Still he didn't open the package or say anything.

The room was getting far too warm. Sophie said to Joe, "It's too early to be choosing bunks. I don't know about you people, but my stomach thinks it's been marooned on a desert island. I suggest we all pile in the car and find a place to eat."

"Hamburgers!" cried Sky.

"Let Eden choose," said Joe. "What do you want, Eden? Pizza? Chinese food? Seafood?"

"Say hamburgers!" insisted Sky.

Eden didn't say anything. His eyes slid sideways in quick, nervous glances, but the rest of him didn't move a muscle.

Sophie said quietly, "Eden, would you like to have hamburgers?"

He gave several big, deliberate nods.

"You don't have to do what Sky wants!" Hannah was shouting. "You can go anywhere you like. It's your choice."

He's not deaf, Mikey wanted to tell her. But then everyone was moving, and Eden was being pushed out the door by a tidal wave of family. "Poor kid," thought Mikey. "He doesn't know what's hit him."

For the rest of the evening, everyone threw conversation at Eden, and he batted it away with shrugs, nods, and headshakes. When they got to the restaurant he got some money out of his pocket and tried to give it to Sophie for his meal. Sophie thanked him and told him to put it back.

This was their treat. He stood beside her at the counter and pointed to order a cheeseburger and fries.

Mikey looked around the place. There was a lot happening—the usual groups of families and kids who just got out of the movies, two birthday parties with hats and balloons, and a baby in a high chair mashing up hamburger and throwing it on the floor. Just about everyone was doing three things at once—talking, laughing, and eating. But not Eden. No way. He was keeping his head down and not making a squeak of any kind. Mikey couldn't believe the way he ate his cheeseburger: one layer at a time like a sandwich cookie. He didn't touch his fries. On the seat beside him was Hannah's box of chocolate walnut fudge, unopened.

Because it was a cold night, Mikey had ordered a hot apple pie for dessert, but when he saw Sky's caramel sundae, he realized that the weather was not a good reason for choosing food. He imagined the thick, rich taste of the caramel against the smooth ice cream, and he said to Sky, "I'll swap you half of mine for half of yours."

Sky shook his head and dug his spoon in deep.

"Come on. It's good. Look, real apples."

"No!" said Sky; then he poked out his curved tongue to show Mikey a mess of caramel and ice cream.

Mikey leaned toward him and breathed out slowly.

"That's not fair!" yelled Sky. "Joe? Sophie? Mikey's blowing germs all over my sundae!"

"Oh Mikey!" Sophie said.

"I'm not! I'm just breathing." He exhaled to demonstrate. "Do you want me to stop breathing?"

"He's doing it again!" Sky covered his ice cream with his hand.

"I'm not doing anything!"

"He is! He's mad because I won't give him half."

"Big deal!" said Mikey.

Sophie said, "Mikey, you wanted apple pie. That's what you got. Don't bug him."

"Why don't you just go and buy yourself a sundae," said Hannah.

Mikey closed his mouth. He wanted a sundae, but saving for a model train was more important.

Silently, Eden slid his hand across the table. For a second his cat eyes looked fully at Mikey; then he nudged some money against Mikey's hand.

Everyone, including Mikey, cried, "Oh, no, no, take it back."

Joe said, "Eden, Mikey has his own money. He just doesn't choose to spend it."

Hannah laughed. "He doesn't spend anything. Mikey's pockets are so deep his dollars bite his ankles and leave teeth marks."

"I'm saving for a train set," said Mikey.

The money sat on the table. Eden had his head down and was as still as a statue.

Sophie put her hand on Joe's arm, and Joe said, "Eden? Thanks. I think you've just saved Mikey's life, Sky's sundae, and our sanity. Mikey will gratefully accept your offer."

Mikey wanted to say no, he didn't want a sundae now, it would choke him, but he saw Sophie's warning look, and he picked up the money. "Thanks, Eden," he muttered, wanting to add, "Yeah, thanks for nothing!"

Eden didn't look up but continued to stare at the table with a face like stone.

Mikey thought he was just about the shyest kid he had ever met. Or maybe the dumbest. Or the cleverest. It was difficult to figure out someone who didn't talk.

It was the same back at the cabin. Do you want to play cards, Eden? Shake, shake. Want a cup of hot chocolate? Shrug. Which bed are you going to sleep in? Shrug again. Are you tired? Nod, nod.

Eden went to the bathroom and came back in yellow pajamas decorated with guitars and music notes. He carried his clothes neatly folded on top of the box of fudge, which was still wrapped, and his sneakers with the socks tucked inside them.

"Hey, Eden!" said Hannah. "Really cool pj's!"

He didn't react but stood there waiting for someone to choose a bed for him. Joe directed him to one of the top bunks, and he climbed up, put his clothes and shoes on the end of the mattress, wriggled into the sleeping bag, and closed his eyes. No goodnight. Nothing.

The next morning, everyone was quiet. The crunch of cornflakes was the only sound at breakfast. Joe, Mikey, and Hannah packed the supplies and cleaned the cabin while Sophie and Sky took Eden back to the home.

Later, they drove north on a fogbound road, talking about other things. Sophie wondered if she had left enough food out for Fatcat. Sky said he had another loose tooth. Joe told Mikey that if he was serious about saving money for a train set, maybe the first thing would be to make an eel trap. Good money in eels. The charter fishing boats in Havelock were always looking for eel bait.

Sophie thought it would be possible to set up a train in the garage. Perhaps a big sheet of plywood could be hauled up to the roof on pulleys when it wasn't being used.

"Why not the house?" said Hannah. "Cut holes in the walls for tunnels! A railroad through the country of Domesticus, stopping at Skytown and Sophieville. Tracks under beds and in and out of closets, along the curtain rods. It's morning. You're lying in bed. Choo! Choo!

Here comes the 7:30 A.M. steam train from Kitchenberg with cars full of toast and puffed wheat. Choo! Choo! Hey Sophie, who was the artist who painted trains coming out of walls?"

"Magritte," said Sophie. "Did I tell you I knew of a man who had a model railway under his house? The neighbor's dog found it. It was chew, chew, all right."

Joe said, "We probably could build it in the garage. We'll look at that possibility."

Sky was unwilling to let go of Hannah's story. He shouted, "In the house, in the house, giving rides to a mouse!"

From there, they all chanted the train rhymes they remembered. Joe said, "Engine, engine, number nine, running along the calico line. Then the line began to shine. Engine, engine, number nine."

Sophie said, "Piggy on the railway, picking up stones. Along came the engine and broke Piggy's bones. 'Oh!' cried Piggy, 'That's not fair!' 'Oh!' said the engine driver, 'I don't care!'"

Mikey told them his favorite. "The peanut sat on the railway track. Its heart was all a-flutter. An engine came around the bend. Toot! Toot! Peanut butter!"

They liked that. They all repeated it, and when they got to the "toot toot" part, Joe hit the horn twice. At once, an oncoming truck tooted back, and they got a wave from the driver. As the truck zoomed past, Sky said it was full of peanut butter, but Mikey was sure he made that up.

The fog was now clearing, and a watery yellow sun was lifting steam from the edges of the road.

Sophie stopped laughing. She looked at Joe and said, "He haunts me!"

No one said anything. They all knew who she meant, just as they knew they couldn't go much farther without talking about him. A feeling of disappointment and failure came and settled in the car like a heavy weight.

Joe said quietly, "I forgot to tell you. His sleeping bag was wet."

Sophie's eyes went glassy with sympathy. She said, "In all my life, I've never met such a lonely child."

CHAPTER FOUR

Rescuing Eden wasn't as easy as Hannah had supposed. In the month after the first meeting, Sophie and Joe had to go to Christchurch twice to talk with Social Welfare officers and Eden's counselor. Hannah thought those people would jump at the chance of getting Eden into a really good family, but it didn't work like that. Everything went in slow steps. Now a Mrs. Parkes from Social Welfare had arrived to look at where and how they lived, and that slightly worried Hannah. Suppose their house wasn't good enough? It was old. They didn't have a television or a microwave oven or a dishwasher. What about the chickens that came in the back door to steal the cat's food, sometimes leaving their droppings on the floor? What about the hole in the porch window, covered over with brown paper? Nothing was ever really tidy. They all tried, but with Joe and Sophie untidy, too, it was difficult to make the place look organized.

Mikey was the neatest in the family, and even he managed to hit the kitchen like a tornado every time he baked anything. He'd made Mrs. Parkes his famous scones to eat with strawberry jam and cream, but he had left a mess. Bowls, flour, milk, the eggbeater covered with cream, dribbles of jam, and cookie sheets covered the counter.

Mrs. Parkes didn't look too hard at the mess. She had come on a Saturday, she said, so she could talk to the whole family. She didn't mention Eden. She seemed more interested in them and what they did. She also liked Fatcat, who purred adoringly at her. He was a real slob, that cat. He jumped up on any lap big enough to take him and then purred like an old tractor, pretending he didn't do this to anyone else. Mrs. Parkes fell for it. As she fed him cream from her finger, she said, "You don't have a TV?"

"No," said Joe. "We don't have time for it."

"What do you do in the evenings?"

"Books mainly," said Sophie. "Hobbies, games, radio, music. Sometimes we are a family orchestra—two guitars, two recorders, and Sky plays a comb and waxed paper."

"What about shopping?"

"What about it?"

"Do you have a local shopping center?"

Joe laughed. "This is the Sounds. We shop from the sea and the land. If we want other things, we drive for two hours on that winding, dusty road to the stores in Picton or Blenheim.

"We keep a town list," explained Sophie. "Every time we need something we write it down, and when the page is full, we have a day out shopping in town."

"So there isn't even a shop by the school?"

"No. Why do you ask?"

Mrs. Parkes smiled and scratched Fatcat under the chin. "You're lucky to live in such a beautiful and remote part of the country. Well, I don't think I need to keep the children any longer. Perhaps they'd like to go outside and play."

Mikey and Sky were away like a couple of rabbits. They were going into the bush by the creek to get supplejack vines to make an eel trap, they said. They could be away for ages. They'd need to take some extra scones in case they got hungry.

Hannah took scones, too, a couple of dry ones in her pocket for Gladly. But she didn't go immediately to the horse paddock. She shut the back door, leaned against it, and listened. She heard Mrs. Parkes say, "Shoplifting has been a problem."

"Recently?" Sophie's voice.

"Oh yes. It's been going on for ages. He doesn't really need the things he takes."

"He won't find much temptation here," Joe said.

"Yes. That's good. All the same, if you're taking him to town…"

"We understand," said Joe.

"We have asked him why he does it. He doesn't seem to know."

Outside the door, Hannah smiled at the woman's lack of understanding. What was it about growing up that made people forget their own childhood? Any kid would know why Eden stole things from stores. He had to. Children couldn't just be—like trees or stones. They had to *do*. If you didn't *do*, then you were invisible to yourself. You were nothing. Some adults took all the doing away from kids. They expected kids just to *be*, like pieces of furniture. When that happened, kids had to go out and do something to save themselves from disappearing.

Hannah had to move. The two pet lambs had come running around the house. When they saw her, they started bleating for bottles of milk. She put on her boots and left before someone could come out to investigate the noise.

She ran in the direction of the hillside paddock. The grass was still soggy from last night's rain, and small rivulets, no wider than her feet, flowed like tears down the wrinkles of the land. Exactly two weeks ago their first lamb had been born. Now there were sheep and lambs everywhere, ewes chewing in the sun, lambs butting and waving their tails in a frenzy of drinking.

The farm looked like a postcard of lambs and daffodils.

In the stream valley where the boys were cutting supplejacks, the bush was glistening with spring green wetness, as though a tide had come up in the night and washed over it. Clematis flowers hung white as snow over dark manuka, and tree ferns put out brown, hairy fists of new growth. Hannah breathed deeply, taking in not just the magic air but the beauty that was in it. She could feel the whole bay, shining blue and green, spiraling down her windpipe and filling up her lungs. She had daffodils and gulls inside her, and long stems of white clematis flowers wound around the red energy of her heart.

Oh! How she wanted to give this special magical bay to Eden! She would show him all its secrets: the bank of glowworms by the creek, the grave of her old horse Shadrach, the trees where the shags nested, the beach cave that boomed at a high spring tide. She'd show him where and how to look for purple tree-fuchsia berries, mushrooms, flounder, spotties, freshwater crayfish and eels, watercress, cockles and pipi, and big old mussels that had pearls inside them. Eden would never be lonely again.

She imagined him rowing and fishing, working on the mussel farm, feeding pet lambs, and telling stories around a bonfire on the beach.

With each new picture he grew, until he was tall and strong, with a smile that outdazzled the sun. She crossed her fingers, a habit she'd had since she was Sky's age, and said to the bay, "You can do it for him!"

She stopped at the horse paddock gate and took another deep breath. Then, filled with sudden energy, she did three cartwheels across the grass. On the fourth, she lost her balance and fell.

She lay on her back in the wet grass, feeling the coldness of the earth seeping through her shirt. She could smell daffodils and sheep and the faint salt of the sea, all mixed like the ingredients of a cake. But she didn't sense Gladly until the filly's head was directly over hers, blocking out the sun.

"Gladly!" She stood, reaching for the pocket of her jeans where the scones had been crushed by her cartwheels. Gladly didn't mind a handful of crumbs. She mouthed Hannah's open hand, her muzzle as soft as fresh raspberries.

Hannah thought she needed brushing again. She was losing her winter coat, which was rough with loose, coppery hair. She was going to be a big horse. She had grown so much since her arrival that Hannah could barely reach across her back. She had Shadrach's broad shoulders, Shadrach's eyes and muzzle; but whereas Shadrach had been quiet and slow-moving like a large sailing ship on a calm sea, Gladly was a nickering, snorting, prancing, dancing machine. She was electric with movement, flickering all over with energy even in her rare still moments. Hannah always felt that she was leading a gale-force wind on the end of the rope. It was hard work. But it was important to lead Gladly every day. At the end of next year, she would go from halter to bridle and bit.

The new halter looked good on her. The first day she had worn it, Hannah had led her to the paddock where Shadrach was buried. She was not sure why she had wanted to show Gladly her father's grave. Maybe it was a desire to show Shadrach the beautiful daughter he had created, and to say thank you. Ritual was important to Hannah.

She had not been prepared for Gladly's reaction. Although the grave had flattened and become overgrown with foxgloves and bracken, Gladly refused to go near it. She whinnied in terror. It was almost a scream. Then she pulled the rope right out of Hannah's hand. Snorting madly, her ears laid back and her eyes rolling, she plunged toward the fence with such speed that Hannah thought she would go into the barbed wire and injure herself. But then she veered away and galloped around the paddock, tossing her head from side to side as though she were trying to shake something off it. Hannah had never before seen a horse behave like that.

Even when Gladly was back in her own paddock, she would not settle down but stood quivering, breathing heavily, and showing the whites of her eyes.

Joe said, "Cows are the same. They get spooked by death."

"But Shadrach's been dead nearly two years. It doesn't even look like a grave."

"It can be longer than that," said Joe. "On the farm when we were kids, we once buried a cow near the path to the milking shed. It was a bad mistake. We couldn't get the rest of the herd near it. So we made a new path, thinking it would be only temporary. Nope. Five years later, we still couldn't get them on the old path by the grave. They'd bellow with heads down, tails up, and yet some of those cows hadn't even been born when the grave was made. The spot looked no different from the rest of the farm."

"What is it that scares them?"

"Beats me," said Joe. "They must have a sense we miss out on. Just goes to show. Humans think they know it all. Fact is, we only know what we take in through our human senses—seeing, smelling, hearing, and so on. We go around making these sweeping statements about the universe—it's this and it's that. What we should be saying is that we see it as this or that. Maybe animals see it in a completely different way."

Hannah thought about it. "How different?"

Joe grinned. "Don't ask me. Look, we go through life learning. When we've learned so much that we're like over-stuffed encyclopedias, we break into real knowledge—knowing how little we actually know. That's what education does for us."

Hannah, who was passionately fond of discovering new things, felt confused. "But it's important to learn."

"Absolutely!" said Joe. "People are made with a hunger for the three big L's—living, learning, and loving."

"You just said learning was useless."

"No! No, I didn't! Do you know how much learning you have to do before you discover your own ignorance? Plenty. And I tell you, Hannah, that discovery brings a good feeling."

"What sort of feeling?"

"Oh, a kind of coming home feeling. Like finding your right place at last. You'll know when you get there. In the meantime, never presume that you know more than the other creatures on this planet. You've read Mark Twain?"

"Yes."

"Mark Twain said, 'Man is the highest creation. Now, I wonder who found that out?'"

Hannah liked that quote. Today she repeated it to Gladly as she led her down the driveway, past Mrs. Parkes's car, and toward the road.

"Do you think horses are the highest creation? I bet you do. You are the princess, and I am your servant to run after you with apples and bread and scones. I brush you and give you hay. I bet you think you have me well-trained."

Gladly walked readily enough across the gravel on the road, but when she got to the bigger stones of the beach, she started fussing and high-stepping.

"All right, girl, take it slowly." Hannah stopped and patted her. "You'll get used to it. I'm going to show you some stuff called sea. Your father couldn't get enough of it. When we were little, he'd wade right out and we'd dive off his back. Then we'd paddle around, catch hold of his tail, and pull ourselves up on his back again. He always watched us. We reckon he used to laugh at us."

She got Gladly as far as the water's edge and that was it. All the talk in the world wouldn't get her farther. The filly sniffed at the sea, which lay against the stones, smooth and waveless, and then pulled back, dragging Hannah with her. Hannah groped in her pocket for the last crumbs of scone, but nothing could persuade Gladly to go near the water. They moved back up the beach, Gladly jittery and Hannah feeling disappointed. It was Shadrach's eyes that looked at Hannah, Shadrach's lips that parted in a whinny of protest. Shadrach had loved the sea.

She was taking Gladly across the road when she saw a yellow pickup truck. The driver was Mrs. Gerritsen, who was married to Mr. Gerritsen, teacher and principal of the tiny Waitaria Bay School. Mrs. Gerritsen taught at school if another teacher was sick, but what she enjoyed most was working with horses. She had three of her own, and she had promised to break in Gladly when the filly was two years old.

As Mrs. Gerritsen stopped the truck, Hannah called out to her, asking what she should do to get Gladly into the sea.

Mrs. Gerritsen got out and ran her hands over the filly, feeling her back and legs. "Some horses do, some don't. You'll have to let her decide. Big girl, isn't she? Looks like a painting of a medieval war horse. Except for the muzzle. That's pure Clydesdale."

"She's so high-strung," said Hannah. "Not quiet like Shadrach. She fights me."

"That's the thoroughbred in her." Mrs. Gerristen took the halter and examined Gladly's mouth. The filly tossed her head and did her usual shake and dance. "Yes, she's spirited, all right. But you have to remember that Shadrach was already old when you got him. He'd have been more lively at this age." She handed back the rope and got in the truck. "Hannah, Gladly is not her father and not her mother. She's herself."

"I know, I know."

Mrs. Gerritsen smiled. "No horse could ever be like Shadrach. You wouldn't want that, anyway. Gladly is special because she is Gladly."

Hannah nodded and smiled.

"Your mom and dad mentioned we might be getting another pupil at the school."

"Yes. Eden. He's a kind of cousin, but we don't know for sure when he's coming. Oh, Mrs. Gerritsen, he's had such an awful life."

"Yes, your mom told me," said Mrs. Gerritsen, who had never gotten used to Hannah, Mikey, and Sky calling their parents by their first names. "It's a brave thing your family is doing."

"Brave? Oh no! We don't think of it like that. It just—it has to be done, that's all. He has really suffered. His mother is dead. No one wants him. He's half-starved…" She stopped, remembering the designer clothing and expensive watch. "He desperately needs a family."

"I can't think of a better family for him, and he'll be very welcome at the school. It'll bring the enrollment up to 49. Mr. Gerritsen is going to talk to everyone and make sure Eden feels at home in class, too. What are his special interests?"

"I don't know," Hannah was quiet for a moment. "His counselor says he likes watching TV."

"Oh well, he'll find plenty to interest him in this place. Maybe he'll look after Gladly for you when you go away to high school next year."

Hannah pulled Gladly closer and put her arm over her neck.

Mrs. Gerritsen asked, "Is she still biting?"

Hannah nodded.

"You know the cardboard tube inside a roll of paper towels or aluminum foil? Tap her on the nose with one every time she nips. She'll soon get the message. Bye, Hannah. See you Monday."

The yellow truck revved away through puddles, and Hannah took Gladly up the driveway. Because Mrs. Parkes's car was still there, she made a detour, leading Gladly down to the creek, where Mikey and Sky were crashing around with their supplejack vines.

Gladly knew the creek and walked easily down the narrow sheep path under the manuka trees. Hannah let the rope go, and the filly went ahead to drink at the stream.

Mikey and Sky had cut several lengths of vine, lashed them together with flax, and put them in the creek to soften.

"How are you going to make an eel trap?" asked Hannah.

"Joe's going to show us," said Mikey. "He says it's like a basket with a funnel in it."

"Round like a wheel," said Sky. He began to sing. "I am an eel trapped in a wheel. How does it feel to be an eel in a wheel?"

"No big deal," said Hannah, and they laughed.

She kicked off her boots and waded into the creek while Gladly munched on mahoe leaves. The water was icy cold and full of light as it splashed from one level of rocks to another. Ferns and mosses made gardens at the edges, and the remains of dead leaves were swept along the current like tiny wrecked ships.

Hannah turned over stones, looking for koura (small freshwater crayfish that hid in crevices and under weeds). Instead, she found the tooth of a sheep, white bone streaked with green. It reminded her of the stories she used to tell about Hannibal Megosaurus, a sheep skeleton that had disappeared from a rock in a creek soon after they buried Shadrach. There had been other stories since, imaginings that had become real with the telling, but none of them had been as powerful as the tale of the great Hannibal Megosaurus, guardian of Shadrach. She dried the sheep's tooth against her shirt. Maybe it was Hannibal's, maybe it wasn't. She would put it on a cord and wear it around her neck.

"Joe called the man in Havelock," Mikey called.

"What man?"

"About the eels. We put them in the freezer until we have a lot, and then we take them in. The charter boats use them for bait. I'll get fifty cents a pound."

"Bait?" said Hannah. "That's a waste of good eel."

"Not when it buys a train set," Mikey said.

Hannah looked toward the house. She could hear the sound of a car in low gear, clutch slipping. She thrust wet feet into her boots. "Mrs. Parkes. She's leaving."

"So?"

She picked up Gladly's rope. "So at last we find out when Eden is coming."

Mike and Sky began to chant softly, "Edenitis, Edenitis, Edenitis."

"Stop that!" Hannah yelled, making Gladly jump.

Mikey laughed. He said to Sky, "I wonder if it's catching?"

"Knock, knock," said Sky.

"Who's there?" grinned Mikey.

"Eden."

"Eden who?"

"Eden I'm scared of getting Edenitis."

Hannah, who was halfway up the sheep path, turned. "You two will regret this!"

Mikey stopped laughing. He shook his head. "No," he said. "You will."

CHAPTER FIVE

A week later, they brought the wet supplejack up to the house and made an eel trap on the picnic table in the backyard. The pet lambs kept getting in the way. The hens picked at the vines. Fatcat, who never ran out of curiosity, sniffed everything and then lay on his back on the table, waving his paws and purring for attention.

Joe twisted the vines and bound them together with fishing line. He made it look easy. First he made a shape like a large, bottomless cup and then wove the body of the trap around it like a large drum. Mikey tried, but the wooden vines, each as thick as his thumb, sprang away like whips or else refused to bend. It was easier when Sky helped him hold the coils.

Under Joe's supervision, they finished making the trap. Then Joe showed them how to use it.

"You put your bait in here. The eels swim through the opening and can't get out again."

"How do we get them out?"

"Put your hand in." Joe demonstrated by pushing his hand through the tunnel opening and grabbing an imaginary eel. He saw their faces and laughed. "When we were young, we used to catch eels by putting our hands in the holes. Yep, that's right. I'd have a fishhook on a string around my wrist. I'd feel along the riverbank for the hole in the mud, and if there was an eel inside, I'd hook it and pull it out."

Sky said, "Didn't you ever get bitten?"

"Once or twice. The little ones weren't too much trouble, but if you got a big one you needed help. Once I put my hand into a hole and there was an eel with a head as big as a sheep's. It was so big my hand wouldn't go around it. I said to it, 'Peace, brother!' and I went on my way." Joe turned the eel trap over. "When do you want to try it out?"

Mikey said, "I thought we'd wait a few days—until Eden comes."

"Edenitis!" muttered Sky.

"It is not!" hissed Mikey, shoving him with his elbow.

"What's that?" said Joe.

"Nothing."

"All right. We'll go down to the river next week. The moon'll be better then for eeling. Maybe we could make a night of it—a family outing. But remember, I get the pick of the eels for eating."

"Sure," said Mikey. "Fifty cents a pound?"

"Fifty cents a pound," said Joe.

The eel trap stayed on the picnic table while the family made other preparations. They shifted the two sets of bunks in the boys' room to make space for another chest of drawers for Eden's clothes.

Sophie told Sky he would have to sleep in the top bunk.

"You know about Eden's problem," she said. "It's not every night, just occasionally, and I'm not climbing a mountain to change a wet bed. Okay?"

"Yeah, yeah, ziggy-bob, yeah. I get the top bunk. Yeah, yeah, yeah."

"I remember when you two wouldn't sleep in the bottom bunks," said Sophie.

"I said I would," replied Sky.

"As long as you don't feel deprived."

"What's deprived mean?"

"It means that I don't want you playing the martyr," snapped Sophie.

He grinned, "What's a martyr?"

Sophie gave a huff of annoyance and walked out.

Sky shrugged at Mikey. "She's being really strange."

"Just wait until tomorrow night!" said Mikey.

"She's got a bad attack of Edenitis," Sky said. "By tomorrow night she'll have spots and dots

and chills and ills and wheezles and measles
and…"

"Sky, please shut the hole in your face. You're
causing a draft."

"I wasn't saying anything!"

"I know. It was pure nonsense!"

Sky was hurt. "You're just as bad with Edenitis."

"I am not!"

"What about waiting to set the eel trap?"

"Sky, I'm sick of the subject! Will you just
drop it?"

"Okay. Thud! There you are. I dropped it, and
it made a hole in the floor." But as they
went out to the kitchen, Sky started again. "Anyway, what about you making him a special
whatchamacallit cake?"

Mikey stopped and folded his arms. "For two
years I've been asking if I can make a Black Forest cherry cake. Two years! Now, at long last, they
buy the chocolate, they buy the cherries, they say
yes. It's got nothing to do with Edenitis!"

Sky's expression shifted. He was thinking of
chocolate and cherries. "Can I help? Please?"

"No! Remember what happened to the chocolate chip dough?"

"I promise, I won't! Look! Cross my heart and
hope to die!"

Mikey hesitated. "All right, but on one con-
dition: You have a piece of tape over your mouth."

The next morning, Joe left for Christchurch before sunup. Mikey heard the car as part of his dream and then woke with the stars outside his window and the sounds of Sophie working in the kitchen. For a while he lay warm in the dark cocoon of his bed, listening to the close whistle of Sky's breathing. Then he remembered yesterday afternoon, and a warm sun of pleasure rose over the horizon of his mind. The Black Forest cherry cake had worked out exactly like its colored picture—even better, because a photograph didn't have the smell of rich dark chocolate and cherries. Nonetheless, the photo in the book had given Mikey the idea of getting Joe's camera to take a picture of his own cake. It was as much art as a painting, or Hannah's stories, or Joe's wood carving, or Sophie's Fair-Isle homespun sweaters, but it didn't last as long. It didn't last at all. It had taken hours to make. Tonight, in a few minutes, it would be reduced to a smudge of crumbs. Still, now that the family knew he could do it, they would probably let him make another one.

That afternoon, Mikey's class went up the hill behind the school for drawing. Most of the children sketched the bay, the hills, the sea, the moored boats, and seagulls like V's in the sky. Mikey drew a picture of his Black Forest cherry cake.

Everyone at school seemed to know about Eden. Mr. Gerritsen had set up a spare desk next to Mikey's and, in the afternoon, someone wrote WELCOME EDEN on the blackboard.

Mr. Gerritsen smiled when he saw the sign. "We don't know that Eden will be at school tomorrow. He might need a day or two to settle in. But it's a very nice thought, and we'll leave the welcome there until he comes."

It had also gotten around the school that Eden's mother had drowned. In the Sounds, drowning was a word that everyone lived with. Parents used it as a threat every time their children fished off a jetty or went out in dinghies without their life jackets. No pupil in the history of the school had actually drowned, although nearly everyone had had a scare at some time—falling out of a boat, swimming out too far, getting caught in a riptide. Now the pupils felt that they were close to a real drowning, even if it had been in a river, and they wanted to know the details. They kept asking Mikey questions as he walked out to the school bus. He couldn't tell them anything. All he knew was that the whole school was suffering from Edenitis.

That afternoon, soon after four, Joe phoned from Blenheim to say they were on the way home.

Sophie said into the phone, "How's it been?" There was a pause and she said, "Oh well, that's to be expected, poor little kid. You'd better get him something before you get on that winding Sounds road."

Mikey and Sky set the table while Hannah picked more flowers, made more cards, and cut a welcome banner to go on the back door. Earlier, she had made a wreath of apple and quince blossoms to go around Gladly's neck, which was, Mikey thought, going too far. Gladly had solved the problem by eating the wreath.

Joe and Eden came in late. They had stopped often because Eden was carsick. When he came in, his skin was greenish white, even the freckles pale. They sat him down, and Sophie poured him a glass of lemonade to settle his stomach. The cards and the flowers were forgotten.

"It's a terrible road!" cried Hannah, who had never suffered from motion sickness in her life. "It's like driving along the back of a never-ending snake—dusty in summer, muddy in winter, bends and bumps, bumps and bends. Oh, you could just die the whole terrible two hours of it, couldn't you, Mikey?"

Mikey nodded, but he remembered that not long ago she had been praising the road for its beauty. Quail, possums, weka, wild pigs, goats, and deer used it more often than cars, she had said. It was one of the few pioneer roads left in the country. What could they do to protect it from change?

Now she was holding her stomach and rolling her eyes. Mikey smiled and felt protective of her.

Eden was still communicating with shrugs, nods, and shakes, but it wasn't long before his freckles regained their color and Mikey could show him around the house while the others put supper on the table. It wasn't a big house—three bedrooms, bathroom, laundry, a kitchen that went into a dining and living area—but it had many interesting things in it. Mikey pointed to the treasure on the wall of the bedroom. There was the shark's jaw, a white pointer caught out near Beatrix Bay, some posters of Maori art from the National Museum, shelves with Sky's rock collection, some papier-mâché dinosaurs they'd made last winter, a photo of himself aged six with a twelve-pound snapper he'd caught, and a wall hanging woven by Sophie from the fleece of Sky's pet lamb.

Eden looked with quick movements of his cat-like eyes but didn't say anything.

"This is your bunk." Mikey patted. "They got you a new comforter."

The boy nodded.

"When you unpack, this is the chest of drawers where you'll put your things. I'll clear some space in the bookcase. See the wooden boxes under your bunk? We have one each. When we were little, they were our toy boxes, but now Sophie's put lids on them, and they're more like treasure chests for our special things. Hannah said you could have hers. It's the purple one. Sky's is blue, surprise, surprise, and mine's green. Look, I'll show you." He pulled out the green box and opened it. "My fishing knife with the deer-antler handle. My great-grandfather's pocket watch. It doesn't work, but one day I'll get it fixed. My old doll I got when I was four, and a double-decker bus that used to be Joe's."

Still Eden didn't speak. He looked, but his face held no expression at all, and his mouth had a slack, unused look. Mikey was feeling the heaviness of pushing a one-way conversation. He closed his box, slid it under the bunk, and said, "I think dinner's ready."

Sophie had cooked mutton stew with watercress and little parsley dumplings. Eden didn't eat much. He kept pushing his fork around his plate and nodding or shrugging, his half-smile flitting in and out. Every time Joe said, "Now, Eden, remember, we want you to make yourself at home," the nod and half-smile came together.

For all his silence, he was eager to be helpful, passing the salt and pepper and getting up to clear the table. Hannah, who was all over him in the biggest display of Edenitis yet, tried to stop him from stacking the dishes. "Eden, this is your 'welcome to the family' party! You're our guest of honor!"

Sophie said in a slow, deliberate voice, "Thank you, Eden. That's very helpful. It would be nice if everyone showed the same enthusiasm for clearing the table."

Eden froze as though he were being criticized instead of praised and went back to his seat, where he sat and stared at his hands in his lap.

Mikey looked at his family. They were reaching out to the kid, reaching, reaching, not touching, and wondering what to do next. He felt unhappy for them. "They want this to work," he thought, "and it's not going to."

He changed his mind a moment later when Sophie put the Black Forest cherry cake on the table. There was a burst of noise, and although Eden didn't join in the cheering, he smiled a real smile. It was almost a grin, and it changed his face. His eyes disappeared to shining, slanted lines, and they saw his teeth, as white and neat as piano keys.

Hannah cried, "Another cheer for Mikey, the fantabulous, delishamostest chef! Hip-hip hooray!"

Mikey felt warmed by it. His reluctance to cut his beautiful cake disappeared, and he sliced down through cherries and chocolate leaves to cut a large wedge for Eden. This time, the boy did not hesitate. He ate the cake as though he had not had a meal in weeks. Then he sat with his hands on either side of his plate, waiting for another piece.

"He's so small," Mikey kept thinking. "I can't believe he is my age. It's not just that he's short and skinny. He's small in his shyness, in the way he moves, the way he is."

The table was circled with praise. It was truly a marvelous cake, and Mikey did not feel at all modest about the compliments that kept coming his way. They were right. Not many adults would be able to make a cake like that. It needed time, and time was something that grown-ups never seemed to have.

"Awesome, awesome, ziggy-bob, awesome," said Sky, licking his fingers.

Eden had almost finished his second piece.

"If you want," Mikey said to him, "I'll show you how to make it."

Eden froze again, the way a rabbit crouches in the grass, and said nothing.

But later that evening, he did speak. They were sitting on their bunks, waiting for Sky to finish in the bathroom. Mikey had been telling Eden about school when Eden had suddenly looked up at him in a different way. Mikey knew he was going to say something, and he leaned forward to hear.

"Got a cigarette?" asked Eden.

CHAPTER SIX

Mrs. Gerritsen had asked Hannah about Eden's interests. Hannah kept coming back to that question, recognizing a big gap in their knowledge of Eden. While they were eating Mikey's fabulous cake, she had looked around the table and made a list of the things each member of the family liked doing. Everyone had a long list. But she had to stop at Eden. None of them knew what he liked or was good at. Admittedly, it was hard getting information from someone who refused to talk, but until they knew about his hobbies and likes and dislikes, they would not be able to do much for him.

Hannah made an important discovery the next morning at breakfast. A big bumblebee was blundering around the kitchen window. As Sophie opened the window to let it out, the bee flew onto another pane, one that did not open. Sophie tried to flick the bee back with a dish towel but it flew out of reach.

Eden, who had been sitting at the table as quiet as a mouse, got up quickly and went to the window. He cupped his hands against the glass as the bumblebee crawled toward him.

"Eden, dear, don't!" said Sophie. "They sting!"

It was in his hands. He carried it to the back porch and opened his fingers. With a heavy, grumbling, sound the bumblebee flew away over the herb garden.

"That was a very brave thing to do," said Sophie. "But bumblebee stings are very painful. Next time, carry it out in a cloth."

Hannah had been in awe at his gentleness in picking up the bee. His small, thin hands had closed around it so carefully that he could have held a soap bubble and not popped it.

When they finished breakfast, Hannah took him up the hill to meet Gladly. There, the same kind of thing happened. When Hannah whistled, the filly came prancing, tossing her head and skittering around as usual. Hannah warned Eden to stand back. "She can bite. She's a little frisky, especially with strangers."

Eden did take a step backwards, but at the same time he held out his hand, and Gladly sniffed it, her nostrils spread, her lips drawn back. Then she did an unusual thing. She moved right up to him and rested her head on his shoulder.

"Look at that! She likes you, Eden! Oh, that

is amazing! She won't stand for me like that!"

He shrugged and put his hand on Gladly's neck.

Hannah whistled. The filly's ears pricked, her head came up, and she trotted over to Hannah to get her slice of bread.

"You certainly know horses," said Hannah.

He moved his head from side to side.

"But you've been around horses—haven't you?"

Another shake.

"You're so good with her. Would you like to lead her sometimes? I do it every day to get her used to handling. I wouldn't mind if you wanted to help. I know that Gladly would…"

But he was walking back to the house and she was talking to herself. She took a deep breath. Twice now, he had done that. Earlier she had been telling him about Shadrach. When she had gotten to the most interesting part about Shadrach's circus tricks, Eden had gotten out of his chair and walked out of the room. It was as though she had not been there.

He had spoken to Mikey and Sophie and Sky, but only a word here and there. He said "Yeah," when Sophie asked him if he wanted to begin school that day, and when Sky asked him what he wanted in his sandwiches, he had said, "Egg." But he didn't speak the words in a normal way. He seemed to hurl them like stones.

He did not seem shy when he walked onto the school grounds, but he did not talk, either. In class, he ducked his head to avoid questions, giving a brief, sharp sound when an answer was unavoidable.

He had said nothing at all to Hannah, and she was the one who had tried the hardest to make conversation with him. She didn't know what to do to change things. It seemed that he was continually slamming a door in her face.

During the lunch hour, she saw Mrs. Gerritsen and told her about Eden's meeting with Gladly. "I think his interest could be animals. He has this stillness about him. You should see the way he picks up a bumblebee. He's like Saint Francis of Assisi."

By an all too extraordinary coincidence, that afternoon Mr. Gerritsen told them to write an animal story. "Any kind of animal." He smiled at Eden. "And any kind of story. It can be real, or you can make it up."

There was no restriction on the place of writing, either, so Hannah took her pen and story folder to a seat by the tennis court and, calmed by the silence of hills and sea, she began a story about a boy called Adam Appletree who had been a dog in a past life.

He wasn't just any dog. He was a little terrier renowned for his friendly disposition

*toward other animals. He had only one
fault, and it was a lamentable one. He
never stopped barking. "Yap, yap, yap,"
until the other animals thought they
would go insane with the sound of his
voice. When the little terrier died, the
great birthing spirit said, "In the next
life he'll be human, and he'll keep his
friendly manner with the animals, but
he must pay for all his noise. He will be
given only five hundred words in his en-
tire life. He must learn to use them wisely
and never waste a single syllable."*

She stopped there, wondering how to finish
it. Then she thought maybe Eden would see the
story and be upset. She tore the page out, ripped
it into small pieces, and buried it under a clump
of grass. Her gaze went back to the sky, the hills,
the sea, and then down to the road where a
pukeko hen high-stepped along the edge of the
road, flicking her tail. Behind her were two
fluffy black chicks on long red legs. She watched
for a while and then wrote a tragedy about some
pukeko chicks whose mother had been run over
on the road and who were raised in a henhouse
with a flock of hens who despised them.

At the end of the writing session, she went
back to class and passed by Eden's desk to
see his story. He was hunched over a page,

his pencil gripped as though something invisible was trying to pull it away from him. The page was scarcely used. There was only one sentence on it: "My favrit animil is a hors."

Hannah planned to take Eden for a long walk with Gladly after school, but there wasn't time. Everyone was talking eels. For Sophie, it was eels and traps and warm clothing. For Sky, the concern was eels and a bonfire. Joe talked about eels and traps, lines, gaffs. Mikey did not separate eels from trains, and to Hannah that made some kind of poetic sense. After all, eels were much the same shape and size. She imagined them sliding along tracks through the countryside in some fairy tale movie. All aboard! The last eel for Picton leaves in one minute!

The trunk of the car was stuffed with an assortment that looked as though it were bound for the dump. There were the oldest of clothes and boots, newspaper, a grill for the barbecue, and plastic containers of food. There were sacks, spears, bags of possum meat for bait, extra tackle, and flashlights. On top of the car, tied with a rope to the roof rack, was the eel trap.

The river at the head of the Sounds came down from the hills as a vigorous stream to grow fuller, deeper, and then open out quietly on the flat of the land near the sea. Here, near the shore, it formed wide beds of gravel with dark pools that lay under clay banks. At high tide, the pools were deep and brackish. At low tide, some of the eel holes on the bank were exposed. Hannah wondered how the eels went back home when the tide was out.

They left the car on the road and unpacked it, carrying the gear down through tussock grass and manuka to the gravel riverbed where they would make their fire. Eden, in silent determination, carried boxes that were too heavy for him. Everyone protested, but it didn't make any difference. His skinny little legs buckled as he staggered through the long grass with a carton of food. Immediately, he was back for the next big container.

While it was still light, Joe and Mikey set the eel trap, baited with possum meat and weighed down with a stone, farther up the river. It would stay there until morning.

Sophie, Eden, and Sky lit the fire while Hannah walked up and down the riverbank looking for wood. They then sat on a log, watching the smoke curl up to the pale evening sky. The air was clear but cold, and they all wore wool hats and pulled the sleeves of their sweaters down over their hands. On the other side of the bank, the weka made their evening call to each other, a "whoo-oop, whoo-oop," echoing along the river. A couple of bellbirds were chiming in a slow, sleepy way, and farther up the hill they heard the sharp shriek of a plover. Venus, the evening star, was now visible, as clear as a raindrop on a window.

Sophie and Joe unpacked the food, with Eden still trying to help. Hannah wished he wouldn't. It was getting embarrassing. She wished she could say, "Stop trying so hard!" and then, having gotten that far, she would probably add, "If you want to be helpful, talk to us!"

At least, when he was helping he was moving. At other times, he sat so still you'd think he was dead. As Hannah had tried to explain to her friends Debbie Godsiff and Joanna Henderson, Eden looked as though he was watching TV, only the TV wasn't there.

Joe put the sausages on the grill, and they began to spit and sizzle. Sophie cut bread. Eden put six plates in a line and then wrapped a knife and fork in a paper napkin for each. The napkins had neat origami folds, and they were set exactly on the plates, carefully adjusted if they were crooked. As Hannah watched, she got a tight feeling that screwed up her face. She hated it when people fussed over things. She got off the log and buttered the bread for Sophie.

Joe turned the sausages. "Won't be long."

"What about singing for supper?" demanded Sky.

Joe glanced at Sophie, then said, "Oh, I don't know about tonight."

"But we always do!" Sky said.

"Not tonight!" Hannah said to him, trying to mouth extra meaning into the words.

"All right." Joe looked at Eden, whose pale face was like a wedge of marble in the firelight. "Eden, it's an old family custom. Everyone performs before they eat. But we're not dumping this on you, okay? Tonight you can be our audience. Well, who's going to start?"

"Me! Me!" shouted Sky, and Hannah knew he was bursting to tell his new knock knock joke.

Sure enough. "Knock knock."

"Who's there?"

"Arch."

"Arch who?"

"You just sneezed. Are you getting a cold?"

Mikey and Joe sang a sea chantey about a mermaid with a comb and a mirror in her hand. Joe did the actual singing, and Mikey, who didn't know the words, crooned plunk, plunk, plunk, pretending he was Joe's banjo.

It was Sophie's turn. She told one of her horrible jokes. "There was this man who worked in a sawmill, and one day he cut his fingers off. He was rushed to the hospital, and he complained to the doctor that he'd never be able to work again. 'Oh, I don't know about that,' the doctor said. 'These days they can do amazing things with microsurgery. They'll sew your fingers back on so you can be working again in no time.' The doctor stopped. He said, 'You did bring your fingers with you, didn't you?' 'No,' said the man, 'I couldn't pick them up.'"

There was a short silence, then Hannah groaned, and the boys booed.

Joe said, "Sophie, that's really awful."

"I know," grinned Sophie. "That's why I liked it."

Eden was quietly laughing into the collar of his sweater, which made Sophie looked pleased. She offered to tell them another, but it was Hannah's turn.

Hannah, knowing what they expected, let a silence within her gather itself into a story. She looked up at the hills and the curly shapes of trees outlined against the sky. She looked at the darkness spreading like a blanket over the Sounds. She felt as though the slow heartbeat of the earth was coming up through the soles of her feet and into her story space. She took a deep breath. "Once there was a beautiful princess who lived deep in the forest with her enchanted horse."

"What was the horse's name?" asked Sky.

She hesitated. "Sassenach," she said, not knowing what the word meant but liking the sound of it. "And it wasn't only Sassenach who was magic. So was the forest. If you went there during the day, the princess seemed like a beggar girl, and the horse looked old with knobbly bones. The trees were tall and stiff, just old trees covered in moss and lichen. But at night, the princess's rags changed to a gown of moonlight, and she wore stars in her hair. Sassenach changed, too. He became a young, wild thing who could gallop as fast as the wind. He was light like the wind, too. His hooves didn't leave any marks. But it was the trees that were the most amazing. When the sun set, they began to wave, with creaking, grunting sounds. They would pull their roots out like feet to walk, and they would bend their branches as though they were showing off their muscles. They talked among themselves in deep, creaky voices, and what's more, the princess understood what they were saying. Sometimes they would bend right down and lift her up in their branches, right up through their leafy hair so she could gather more stars."

"Sorry, Hannah," said Joe. "The sausages are beginning to burn."

"Oh no!" said Sky who wanted more of this new story.

Hannah wasn't sure what would happen next and was grateful for the interruption. "It's all right. I'll finish it later."

But later there were noises coming from the darkness of the river, an occasional plopping, splashing sound that had Mikey standing and eager to begin eeling. As soon as they were finished and plates packed away, they went down to the water's edge.

Mikey and Joe took a couple of sacks and their homemade spears and walked farther along the river toward the sea. Hannah, Sophie, and Sky unrolled their fishing lines. Eden shook his head. He didn't want to go eeling. He went back to the fire and sat poking it with a stick.

They used possum for bait. Beside the dark pond of the river, beyond the edge of the firelight, Hannah set her flashlight down in the gravel beside her line. She swung the sinker and baited hook, then let go. The line moved out in a slow curve and splashed near the far bank. A little farther away she heard the splash of Sky's sinker. As she bent to pick up the flashlight, Sky yelled, "Bites! Bites!"

"Shh! It's only the current."

"No! Bites! Shine the light!"

She turned, and at that moment her own line pulled, then went slack. "Eels!" she cried.

"Yeah! I told you!"

The flashlight made a round puddle of light on the surface of the river. Under it were long, dark shapes, twisting like strands of seaweed around the bait. The light seemed to make them nervous. They drew back. Hannah turned the flashlight away. "There are dozens of them!"

"Got one!" Sky was hauling on his line. "Help me, Hannah!"

She couldn't do anything, for in that instant an eel struck her own line and pulled it through her hand.

"Sophie!" they both yelled.

Their mother, who did not yet have her line in the water, came running. So did Eden.

Sky pulled his eel out onto the stones, where it curled and uncurled on the line. It was black, shining, more than a foot long.

"We need a stick!" cried Sophie, and Eden passed her the twig he'd been using to stir the fire.

"No! Something bigger!"

Hannah's eel was trying to swim away, pulling like a small submarine. The flashlight showed her line tight as a wire and a V-shaped ripple where it entered the water. Every now and then, the ripple turned into a whirlpool and the line ran through her fingers.

"Sophie! Help me! Mine's huge!"

Eden came back with a thicker piece of wood, and Sophie bashed Sky's eel on the tail. It stopped wriggling, and she dropped it tail first into the sack. She then held the sack around the eel's gills while she took out the hook.

"Sophie!" yelled Hannah, "The line's cutting my hands!"

"Here!" Sophie thrust the sack at Sky. "Tie the top so it can't get out. All right, Hannah, let's see what you've got. Good grief!"

"I said it was huge."

"Huge? It's the Loch Ness monster! Hold the light."

There was a great splashing in the river as Sophie walked backward with the line. The flashlight showed a patch of churning water and the dark curve of something as thick as a car tire.

Sophie kept walking backward until she was near the fire and the eel was up on the gravel. It writhed in the light, knotting itself into dark shining coils, unknotting again. Hannah guessed that it was almost as long as she was tall. It had a large blunt head, and its belly was almost white.

"The wood!" Sophie called to Eden. "Before it gets off the hook!"

Eden didn't move.

Sky dropped his line and ran to fetch the sack and the wooden club. He helped Hannah hold her line while Sophie thumped the eel's tail. It took several blows to stun it. "I'm not putting my hand near this one's mouth," said Sophie. "You're going to have to cut the hook off."

It took all three of them to get the eel into the sack, and when the sack was tied it looked full. The giant eel recovered and began to writhe, moving the sack as though it were in a sack race.

"It'll be all right," said Sophie. "It can't get away now."

The drama over, they laughed and congratulated themselves

"More than twenty pounds," Sophie said. "Probably nearer twenty-five."

"Bigger than any of us have caught before," said Sky. "Hannah, you've got the record. Wait till school tomorrow. You could write a story about it."

Sophie said, "If it had gotten away, Mikey and Joe would never have believed it."

Eden was standing beside the fire, a statue again. His fists were bunched up inside the sleeves of his sweater, and his hat was pulled down almost over his eyes. The light flickered on his tight chin and mouth.

"He doesn't like this," Hannah whispered to Sophie.

Sophie walked over and put her hand on his arm. His shoulder dropped, and he took a step to the side, turning his head away.

"Does it upset you, Eden?"

He shrugged.

"I suppose we're not very sensitive. It's our lifestyle. We do care about all creatures, but at the same time we live off the land and the sea. We catch things and kill things. We don't buy them already killed, in supermarkets." She glanced at the sack. "It doesn't sound very nice, but it's the way things are."

Sky spun his hooks and sinker and let them drop with a plop into the river. Hannah struggled in the poor light to put a new hook on her line.

Sophie was saying to Eden, "I used to think about being a vegetarian. Then I thought, what's the difference between eating a cabbage and eating a fish? It's all the same life energy. It just keeps getting exchanged and taking on different forms—cabbage, fish, me. When I die and get buried in the earth, the worms will have a feast. A bird may eat the worms. A cat may catch a bird. There you are, a bit of Sophie in someone's pet cat." She laughed and turned to walk back to Hannah.

"I've got another one!" yelled Sky.

Sophie whispered to Hannah, "I don't know why I'm talking this way."

Hannah felt the need to defend her mother. She called to Eden, "There are lots of eels in the river. They eat all the trout. We need to catch them. I know hooks look cruel, but you should see what fish do to each other!"

"Sophie?" yelled Sky. "Help me!"

"At this rate," said Sophie, "I won't get my line near the river."

About an hour later, Joe and Mikey came back wet and cold. They had fallen in, but they were carrying two sacks of eels. While they steamed beside the fire, Hannah showed them the eel she called Queen of the River.

"What did you get, Eden?" Mikey asked.

Eden didn't answer. He picked up a box to carry back to the car.

"Not everyone likes fishing," Sophie said. "Why should they? It'd be a dull old world if we were all the same."

Hannah gave Mikey a warning look.

Mikey understood. He glanced at Eden's back and muttered, "If we were the same as him, it'd be a dull world, all right."

"Hush!" Hannah warned.

On the way home, Eden spoke to Hannah for the first time. The four of them were squashed together in the back, Eden sitting forward on the seat, leaning into the gap between Sophie and Joe. Hannah was aware of the sharpness of his bones and the unfamiliar scent of his hair and skin. He wriggled around until he was almost facing her, then said in his hard, bullet-like voice, "You going to finish that story?"

Chapter Seven

Joe told Mikey that work was to be enjoyed for its own sake. "If work only means money to you, you cheat yourself of the pleasure of the job."

Mikey grunted. Joe was always giving them sermons about life, and no one minded too much. Sometimes he said things that were useful. But when you were saving for something that seemed about as expensive as a rocket trip to the moon, it was difficult not to think of work as money. Every time he pulled eels out of the river, he measured them not in inches but in dollars and cents. Nor were the dollars growing as quickly as he had hoped. At first, when the eels had been plentiful, his plans for the model railway had been ambitious. Sometimes the trap had been so full he'd had difficulty getting it up on the bank. But the supply did not last long. It dwindled to a few, then one or two, then none, and he would have to find new places along the river.

Not all the eels were sold in Havelock as bait. Joe picked them over and kept the best for eating. The smaller ones were cleaned, rubbed with a mixture of salt, brown sugar, and spices, and hung in the smokehouse over a slow manuka fire. The bigger eels were chopped up and cooked fresh.

Eden refused to eat them.

Sophie kept the weighing scales on the back porch and wrote down all the figures in the back of her accounting book. Sophie respected money and understood it, which was why she managed the family finances. Mikey thought that Joe, Hannah, and Sky were all messy with money. They treated it as though it had come down the chimney with Santa Claus, and they were always running out. Sometimes they teased Mikey and called him Mikey-Miser and other made-up names because he kept his savings to himself. He wasn't stingy. But if he loaned them money, they would forget to pay him back, and that was more of a nuisance than he cared to handle. Once he'd had to ask Joe four times for the two dollars he had borrowed. Eventually Joe had taken a five dollar bill from his pocket and said, "Take this!" and Mikey had been embarrassed.

It was true that Mikey did like money. He saw nothing wrong with that. He enjoyed the power of it, adding up figures and feeling the power increase. He was also aware that money was very hard to get.

The train fund was at the stage where he could almost afford a basic layout, transformer, figure eight of track, locomotive, a couple of cars, and a caboose. That would be a beginning. But when the eels ran out, he would have to look for some other way of making money.

They each got an allowance, of course, but it wasn't much. His chores were to help with the sheep, split firewood, and keep the bins filled for the woodstove. He also cooked dinner two nights a week.

At the Friday night family conference they all got paid, with deductions made for jobs forgotten or not done properly. Of course, Eden never had anything deducted from his allowance. He liked making things tidy, so Sophie had put him in charge of the toolshed and the kitchen cupboards. He also took over Sky's job of feeding the hens and cleaning out the henhouse.

Eden spent a lot of time at the henhouse, almost as much as he spent with the filly. Every afternoon, he let the hens out to scratch and pick in the grass, and he would bring the eggs in bunched up in the front of his shirt.

Sometimes Mikey watched him with the hens. He could walk up to any one of them and the bird would squat down on the ground, waiting for him to pick it up. No squawking. No ruffling of feathers. He did the same kind of thing with the big bush blowflies that were coming into the house now that the weather was warmer. He would go to the window, put out his bony hands, and carry them outside.

One afternoon they watched him through the kitchen window. He had a hen under one arm and was stroking its neck feathers with his finger.

"He must have the right aura for animals," said Hannah.

"What's aura?" asked Sky.

"Like a halo all around your body," said Hannah.

"Energy field," said Mikey.

Joe explained, "Sky, we're all made of electrical energy. It extends out beyond us…"

"I'm not," said Sky. "I'm made of skin and bone and bloody-blood-blood."

Sophie said, "I don't know. Maybe the attraction is Eden's lack of energy. He is certainly the quietest child I've ever come across."

Mikey could have told them that there were times when Eden wasn't quiet, but if he did, they would want to know what Eden said. Mikey couldn't tell them that. Anyway, it wasn't normal talk. It happened when he and Eden were alone together, Eden throwing words out like spit and watching to see how they landed on Mikey.

Like the time he was sitting on his bunk while

Mikey was doing homework.

"This place is a dump!" he said in his rough, gravelly voice. "Rotten old house. No TV even. It's gross!"

Mikey opened his box of colored pencils and began to fill in a map of New Zealand.

"Everyone else has a TV. My nanna's got twelve TVs."

Mikey swallowed and shaded the coastal areas green.

"She has! She has twelve TVs, and one's got a screen bigger than this wall."

Mikey refused to look up. He worked with his face close to the map, and after a while he heard a creak as Eden lay down on the bunk. There was a soft, thudding noise. Eden was kicking his heels against the mattress.

"No TV! No stores! A real dump! How am I supposed to get any cigarettes?"

The inland areas above sea level were supposed to be colored yellow and the highlands brown. The high peaks were left white.

"I bet you have so smoked," growled Eden. "You can't kid me. I've smoked a pack of cigarettes a day. It's cool, man!"

In his head, Mikey was saying, "Shut-up, shut-up," but he didn't let that show on his face or in the pencil strokes on the paper.

Eden gave up. He went still again and lay on the bunk with his hands at the back of his neck.

He hardly seemed to be breathing.

Mikey had gotten as far as the edges of the Southern Alps when Eden started up again.

"Your sister Hannah—she's a nerd."

He put his head down again, close to the pencil. The pencil lead broke and spun away across the map. A hot feeling came up Mikey's neck and spread across his face. He hated any kind of fighting, but right then he wanted to punch Eden's teeth right down his skinny little throat.

Mikey did not like Eden. He admitted it to himself without the slightest twinge of guilt. Eden didn't like him, either. That was why Eden baited Mikey.

Mikey thought it all through very carefully and decided he had nothing personal against the kid. It was just that Eden didn't fit into the Sounds way of living. He was different. He liked different things. Cigarettes! Yuck! As for TV, Mikey had sometimes watched it at other people's houses, but he wouldn't want to watch it all the time.

It was his job to help Eden with his reading every day after school, but neither of them enjoyed that. Sophie would have to tell them half a dozen times before they put the reading book on the table. They would sit with their chairs far apart.

Sometimes Eden wet his bed. Mikey would wake up to the smell of it and tell himself that this could not possibly last. Sooner or later his family would give in and take the kid back to Christchurch.

So far there was no sign of that happening. He thought that maybe some of their Edenitis had worn off, but Hannah and Sophie still treated Eden like royalty. He only had to do something ordinary like wiping up the cat's milk after Sophie had stepped in it, and she would fall all over him with praise.

"It's pukifying!" Mikey said to Sky.

One day Joe heard Mikey discussing Edenitis with Sky, and he got really angry about it, saying they were not to use that word again. Did they hear?

Mikey nodded. But not saying "Edenitis" didn't take the word out of existence, nor did it prevent it from sounding off in Mikey's head every time he saw them making a fuss.

At school it was different. Debbie and Glen Godsiff, who had caught a dose of Edenitis from Hannah, were still trying hard, but some of the kids were sick of him. He had brought it on himself by the way he ignored them, looking right through them or shrugging and walking away. When he did speak, it was usually to brag about something. Mikey saw the friendship go out of faces one by one as the kids at school switched off. A couple of boys nicknamed Eden "The Weed."

Hannah was aware of this, and it made her doubly protective of Eden at school. She was always hovering around him, she and her friend Debbie.

One morning, Debbie brought to school a new electronic toy her uncle had sent from America. It was shaped like a large clover leaf and had three windows, a different game in each. Everyone was dying to get their hands on it. Kids just about stretched their necks right off to see how it worked. But who was allowed to play with it? Eden. She let him have it all lunch hour, and the rest of them had to stand there listening to it buzzing and beeping.

"Can I have a turn?"

"Come on, Debbie, you're my best pal."

"The Weed's had it for ages!"

One of the boys did try to snatch it, but Hannah and Debbie moved in and the boy backed off. Eden went on pushing buttons as though nothing was happening.

"Hope your batteries die!" someone yelled.

Actually, something worse happened. The game disappeared. That afternoon when Debbie couldn't find it, the children pointed at Eden. "He had it. Ask him."

"I gave it back," Eden said.

"He did, too," said Debbie. "He put it on my desk."

"I saw him," nodded Hannah.

Mr. Gerritsen organized a search of the classroom, and then everyone had to empty out their bags. Mikey looked hard at Eden's things. The game wasn't there. It wasn't anywhere.

"Did you take it outside again, Debbie?" Mr. Gerritsen asked.

Debbie shook her head. Her face was pink, and she was close to crying.

"Don't worry. It hasn't dissolved into thin air," Mr. Gerritsen said. "It'll be out on the playground. All right, everyone. Let's form a search party."

They spread out across the school grounds, hunting from one side to the other: tennis court, swimming pool, the sheds and bathrooms, under seats, and in trash cans. Someone pointed across the road to where the tide lapped high on the beach, and suggested that maybe the game was left down there.

"We'll have another look tomorrow," Mr. Gerritsen said.

Later that afternoon, while Eden was out collecting the eggs, Mikey looked through Eden's things—his school bag, the purple treasure chest, and the dressing table drawers. He felt both guilty and relieved when he didn't find the game. He tried to leave everything as he had found it, but Eden, with his passion for neatness, knew at once that his possessions had been touched. He grabbed his schoolbag, looked inside, and then his eyes accused Mikey.

"I—I wanted to borrow a ruler," Mikey mumbled.

"You think I stole her game."

Mikey scratched the back of his neck and felt miserable. "Well, you did say—remember you told me you stole things?"

"Not now. Not from her."

Mikey met his gaze. The boy was leaning toward him, and his eyes were wide open, as clear as a drink of water.

For once, thought Mikey, he was telling the truth.

Debbie Godsiff's special toy did not turn up the next day or the day after. Mikey knew that many of the kids had wanted to play with it. Maybe one of them had sneaked it down to the beach when she wasn't looking, and the tide had washed it away. Or maybe it had been left on the grass and a weka had taken it.

Eden hadn't seen a weka before coming to the Sounds. He thought it was a kiwi.

"No, the weka—sometimes called a woodhen," explained Sophie. "They hang around the house trying to get the cat's food."

Hannah said, "They're the villains of the bird world. They'll steal anything. We found a weka nest once, and in it were some keys, pencils, a shoe, a plastic bottle, bits of foil, even a beach towel. It's not just food they take. They steal for the sake of stealing…"

"Hannah!" said Sophie. "Come and help with the dishes."

Three days after the game disappeared, there was heavy rain. That put an end to the search. If the sea hadn't ruined it, the rain had. Besides, there were other things to talk about at school—like Mikey's plans to increase his eel business. He knew that there were a number of good eeling rivers in the Sounds, but most of them were too far away for an afternoon bike ride. He decided to hire others in his class. They could fish and gaff the rivers in their own areas, and he'd give them twenty-five cents a pound for their eels.

When he talked about this at the family conference, Joe was not pleased.

"You can't expect me to approve," Joe said. "Your friends do the work for twenty-five cents a pound, and you sell at fifty cents. All that profit for no work."

"That's business," said Mikey. "And it's not for nothing. I organize it. I store the eels in the freezer and take them into Havelock."

"You store them in the family freezer, and we use the family car to deliver them," said Joe.

"So your family is entitled to an opinion. I don't think it's right that you should take advantage of your friends in such a way."

"It's what people do all the time," Mikey insisted.

"Not what we do," said Joe.

Sophie interrupted. "Hold on, Joe. I'm on Mikey's side. This is his enterprise, and I think he should run it his way."

"It's a neat plan," said Sky. "Fantiddlytastic!"

"I can't seen anything wrong with it," said Hannah. "It's not as bad as selling Shadrach to the dog food factory."

"Hannah!" said Sophie.

"We're supposed to be able to say anything we like at family conferences," Hannah said.

"Fine," said Joe. "Which is why I'm saying I don't like the way Mikey is extending his eel industry."

"Then let's put it to a family vote," Mikey said.

Joe tore a page off his notepad and divided it into six. They passed the pencil around and wrote under the cover of their hands. The votes were counted. Four had yes. Two had no.

Mikey glared at Eden, who was sitting like a statue, staring at the table. The Weed had deliberately voted against him.

On Sunday night, Sophie forgot to wake Eden up and take him to the bathroom before she went to bed. Mikey woke on Monday morning with the familiar smell drifting up from the bottom bunk. "Not again!" he moaned. "Poo! What a stink!" And he put the covers over his head.

He thought that Eden might be still asleep, but knew he wasn't when he heard Sky's anxious voice. "It doesn't matter. I used to wet the bed, too, when I was little."

Sky must have told Sophie about Mikey's remark, because when Eden was in the shower, Sophie came like a whirlwind into their bedroom. She was carrying a set of clean sheets. In one movement, she tore off the wet sheets and waterproof mattress cover; then she threw the clean ones down beside Mikey. "All right. You can make his bed. Maybe you'll learn something!"

He opened his mouth to argue, but when he saw how angry she was, he closed it again. He couldn't afford to have her siding with Joe about the eeling business. He folded his arms and waited until she went out.

"And do it right!" she snarled as she sailed down the hallway.

"Rotten Edenitis!" he muttered to himself.

He unfolded the waterproof blanket. It crackled and had a rubbery smell that always got stronger with warm pee on it. He laid it on the mattress and then tried to straighten the sheet over it. As he leaned across the bunk to tuck in the far side, something rattled. It sounded like a loose slat. Kneeling on the edge of the bunk, he reached right over, his head against the wall, so that he could get his arm under the mattress. He groped along the wooden boards, and his fingers touched a flat plastic object. He pulled out Debbie Godsiff's electronic game.

"Sophie?" He marched down to the kitchen, holding it in front of him. "Sophie?" he bellowed.

CHAPTER EIGHT

Gladly's hooves echoed like drumbeats around the bay. The sound was tossed back and forth between the hills, vibrating on the flat green sea and shivering in the leaves of every tree. It went on and on.

"Why does he do that!" Mikey complained.

"It's not Eden," Hannah said. "It's Gladly."

"I know that. But he's the one making her gallop."

"He doesn't," Hannah said. "He just stands in the middle of the paddock. She gallops around him."

"Maybe he hypnotizes her," said Sky.

"Don't be silly," Hannah replied.

"Why not?" said Mikey. "He seems to have hypnotized everyone else."

Drum, drum, drum. The noise made soft explosions in the kitchen, and a bottle on the counter rattled out the rhythm. Drum, drum. Hannah sighed, took two apples from the fruit bowl, and went outside to put on her boots.

Although Gladly was now almost fully grown, her legs still looked too long for her body. Not that her body was small. She was strong, deep-chested, broad in the back, and had a powerful neck. Her mane and tail floated like breaking waves as she galloped around the fence lines, and lumps of earth flew up behind her hooves. All the grass had been worn from the outer edge of the horse paddock, and the dirt was packed hard, grooved as though it were a racing track.

Around and around she galloped, her head rocking, sweat shining on her flanks, while Eden stood in the middle. He was turning so that he was always facing her. It was as though he had her on a long, invisible rope.

Hannah climbed over the fence, put her fingers in her mouth, and whistled.

At least that still worked. Gladly skidded sideways in a shower of dark earth and turned, breaking her gallop to an easy trot. She came up, sniffing for the apples in Hannah's shirt pocket. Hannah took one out and gave it to her. The filly radiated heat like a furnace. Great welts of frothy spittle shivered on her flanks, and she was wet all over.

As Eden approached, Hannah shouted at him, "You have no right to let her run so hard!" But as she said it, she knew it was not his doing. Gladly had been galloping *for* him, not because he had made her do it. That knowledge did not make

Hannah feel better. "Look at her!" she cried.

Eden came over to the horse, his face full of concern. Rarely did he show emotion, but now he looked as though he was going to cry, and Hannah wished she could take back her words. She took the other apple from her pocket, offered it to him, and said, "She'll be all right. Give her this."

But at once Eden got his stony look. He turned and walked away. While Hannah watched his departing back, Gladly leaned across, scooped up the second apple, and nearly took Hannah's fingers as well.

Hannah guessed that Eden had been spending extra time in the horse paddock to avoid being with the family. He was probably still feeling awful about Debbie's game. Well, he wasn't the only one. Debbie was Hannah's friend. Debbie had let Eden play with the toy as a favor to Hannah, and look what he had done. Oh, it wasn't so much the taking of it. It was the ongoing deceit. Eden had actually joined in the search.

It had been all that was needed to turn Mikey against Eden. Everyone else, though, had done their best to smooth things over. Sophie drove down to the school with Eden, explained everything to Mr. Gerritsen and then to the Godsiffs. To Debbie, she said, "Eden has made an error of judgment, and he wishes to apologize."

In school, Mr. Gerritsen announced that the game had been found. That was all. But some students who had been talking with Mikey hissed, "Weed, Weed, Weed, Weed—" until Mr. Gerritsen told them to be quiet and get on with their work.

That day, the only kids who would talk to Eden at school were Hannah, Sky, and the two Godsiffs. Hannah thought that maybe Debbie was so pleased to get her game back that she was more than ready to forgive Eden. Or maybe she was feeling really sorry for him. She made a point of being friendly to Eden in public. After the first bit of awkwardness, Eden seemed pleased. He talked to her more than usual.

He ignored the others, and mostly they ignored him, although some made rude remarks like, "Watch your pocket! Here comes the Weed!"

In the middle of the week, Mrs. Godsiff phoned. She told Joe they were all going to be away the following week. They were going to the North Island for a family wedding. Before they left, they would like to have Eden come over for dinner. Would he be interested in coming Friday night? They'd bring him home about half past eight.

Joe said to Sophie, "Now that's one nice family!"

Sophie put her finger over her lip as a warning.

"It's all right," said Hannah. "He's out with Gladly."

Sophie said softly, "It is extraordinarily generous, I must say. But what if he won't accept?"

"He'd better go!" Joe said.

Hannah smiled. "Oh, he'll go all right. The Godsiffs have a TV."

"I forgot about that," Sophie said.

Joe sighed and shook his head. "You know, it's about the only real conversation I've had with him. When are we going to get a TV? We aren't. Why not? No reception in this place. Couldn't we get it if we put an antenna on top of the hill? Too expensive. Why not sell some sheep to pay for it? Because I'd rather watch the sheep."

"He's still suffering withdrawal," said Sophie. "Mrs. Parkes thought that television became his real world."

"I think it's just because he likes stories, and he can't read well enough to get them out of books," said Hannah.

There was no doubt in her mind that Eden was addicted, not to television but to stories. She watched him as she told stories and saw the tight bud of his face open up like a soft flower. He liked her stories much more than Mikey did, maybe even more than Sky, who wouldn't go to sleep without another episode of the forest princess, the tale she had begun the night of the eeling expedition. Mikey usually lay on the top bunk reading something factual, a book about food or engineering, or how to preserve possum skins, or twenty designs for making a raft. She would sit on the end of one of the lower bunks, her feet tucked under the comforter.

Because Sky had wanted a prince as well, there were now two characters in the story. After a series of adventures, the Princess Raku, on her enchanted horse Sassenach, had discovered her brother Drakmar, who had been kidnapped when he was a baby by some trolls called Doomroths. Having been fed troll soup for most of his life, he had gained troll strength and could run all day without getting tired. He was smaller than his sister but just as beautiful. He didn't have the troll's warty faces and hearts. His own heart glowed golden with a kindness for all living things, even for the Doomroths who had princenapped him.

"What's the name of his horse?" Eden asked.

"He doesn't have a horse."

"He has to. He needs a horse like her one."

"No, he doesn't. I told you. He can run as fast as any horse."

"But he wants a horse!"

"Eden, this is my story. If you don't like it you don't have to listen."

"Why can't Drakmar have a horse?" Sky was on Eden's side.

"Do you want me to go to bed?"

"No! No!"

She breathed deeply, freeing the cramp in her ribs, and finding her way back to the story. "Well, not only can Drakmar run faster than any horse on earth. One day he discovered he could fly."

"Fly?" cried Eden. "You mean real flying?"

There was a rustling sound in the top bunk. Hannah looked up and saw Mikey mouthing something over his book. Not a sound came out but she knew what he was saying. Edenitis. Edenitis.

Hannah didn't know what was wrong with her brother. Mikey had always gotten along with everyone. Like Joe, he was a natural peacemaker who went around trying to patch up friendships. Yet he wouldn't even try with Eden. He ignored him. And Eden, who had times of talk with the rest of the family, avoided Mikey.

Hannah wished her brother could be more understanding.

But that was another thing about Mikey—his stubbornness. Once he set his mind to something, he would not change.

"Thank goodness," Mikey said, when he learned that Eden was going to the Godsiffs' on Friday night. "Can't they keep him?"

Joe and Sophie looked at each other and said nothing.

After two months of Eden day and night, it seemed strange to come home from school without him. It was as though the family had changed shape to fit him in, and now there was a big chunk missing. Even being in the horse paddock without him seemed strange. Hannah mentioned this to Mikey, who was up by the henhouse rubbing slime off eels with salt.

"You've got to be joking!" Mikey said.

"Don't you miss him just a little?"

"Oh sure, the way I miss having the measles."

"Mikey, that's not very nice."

"I'll live with it." He dropped a clean eel into a bucket of water.

"You've changed," said Hannah. "You've really turned against him."

"Me? You've got a short memory. I said right from the beginning I didn't want him to come here. He doesn't belong in our family."

"The problem is, he doesn't belong anywhere. We all knew it was going to be difficult. We thought we'd do our best. We thought we would try…"

"Thought, thought, thought!" cried Mikey, grabbing another eel from the sack. "I tell you what I think! He's a creep! A thieving little liar! And it makes me sick to see the way you're all cozying up to him—even the Godsiffs after what he did to them. It's—it's…"

"Pukifying?" suggested Hannah, trying to make him smile.

"Shut up about him!" Mikey yelled at her. "Just shut up, will you?"

Then Hannah saw that Mikey's shoulders were shaking, and tears had filled his eyes. She put her arm around him. His T-shirt, skin, even his hair, smelled of greasy eel. "Oh, Mikey!" she said.

Mikey rested his head against her. "I hate him!" he bawled.

None of this conversation came out at the family conference. Joe began by saying he realized that the past two months hadn't been easy, especially for Mikey, and he wanted to thank them all for their patience and generosity.

He added, "At the same time, I hope you realize it's been much more difficult for Eden. We all have each other. He has to adjust on his own."

Mikey didn't say anything.

"I think he's adapting very well," said Sophie. "There's been a great improvement in communication."

"He talks to you easily enough," said Joe. "He probably feels more comfortable relating to a woman. He's been used to his mother, grandmother, his aunts. He likes helping in the kitchen."

"He talks to me, too," said Sky. "One day he's going to take me to his stepfather's farm in Australia. He has two hundred horses, and one of them won the Melbourne cup three times."

"He's lying," said Mikey.

Sophie said, "Sky, sometimes when people feel powerless they make up things to impress other people."

"No!" Hannah insisted. "I told you it's because he likes stories. He makes them up—the way I do."

Sophie smiled. "He certainly likes *your* stories. But I don't know what we're going to do about his reading. He's way behind Sky, and that can't be too good for his self-esteem."

Mikey said, "I don't want to help him with his reading anymore."

Sophie asked, "Why not, Mikey?"

Joe stopped the question with his hand. "That's okay. Sure, Mikey, we respect your feelings."

"It's all right. I'll do it," said Hannah. "You know what? I'm going to write down the story of Raku and Drakmar. He likes that. I bet he'll read it."

"Can I read it, too?" asked Sky.

"You'll have to ask Eden," said Hannah. "It'll be his book." As she said it, she glanced at Mikey and saw a look of hate and misery in his eyes.

Joe must have seen it, too. He leaned back in his chair, put his hands behind his neck and said, "Mikey, it's just about time for another trip to Christchurch."

"Christchurch!" Mikey suddenly sat up straight.

"We need to see Social Welfare again. I thought we might make an appointment for next Tuesday."

"Can I come, too?"

"Of course! If the Godsiff children can take a week off school, I'm sure Mr. Gerritsen can spare you for one day. While Eden and I visit Mrs. Parkes, you might like to spend some time in the train and hobby shop."

"I want to come!" Sky was on the edge of his seat. "Please, Joe! Mikey? I helped with some of the eels."

Joe said to Mikey, "What do you think?"

Mikey was now grinning as though he'd swallowed a day full of sunshine. "Let him come with us."

"Why don't we all go?" suggested Hannah.

But Sophie said, "No, at the risk of sounding sexist, I think it would be a good idea if the womenfolk had some quality time at home on their own."

Mikey was adding figures in his mind. "I have enough money!" he said, his eyes shining. "I can buy it!"

CHAPTER NINE

Mikey didn't know how he could wait until Tuesday. His train catalog, new three weeks ago, was now falling to pieces. He knew most of the prices by heart. Still, he kept turning the pages, adding up figures, wondering if there had been any recent price increases.

He asked Sophie if he could have the table in the front room until he got a permanent layout in the garage.

"My weaving loom's on it."

"You could put it away."

"What about my weaving?"

"Sophie, it won't be for long."

Sophie considered. "All right, we'll share the table."

"It's not big enough for a loom and a train!"

"No, silly. We'll take turns. Two weeks for your railway, two weeks for my weaving."

"Thanks, Sophie!" He put his arms around her, and she hugged him, bending down so that her hair fell over his face. It had a good smell, like shampoo and vanilla.

"I know it's been very hard for you, Mikey," she said softly.

"It's okay."

"I'm so grateful to you."

"What for?"

"For everything. For being wonderful. For being my own dear Mikey."

He clasped his hand behind her back and squeezed so hard that she yelped and tickled him, and then they both ran laughing into the kitchen. Then Sophie stopped and gasped, her mood changing.

Hannah and Eden were on the kitchen side of the back door. Between them, half in and half out the door, was Gladly.

"Hannah! Not inside!" Sophie yelled.

"But Shadrach used to come into the house," Hannah said.

"He came in uninvited," Sophie said. "Don't train Gladly to do the same thing. Horses stay outside!"

"I just want her to see where we live."

Mikey thought it was a stupid thing to do. The horse didn't even like being there, front hooves on the linoleum, back feet on the concrete floor of the porch. She shuffled nervously, rolled her eyes, and snorted.

Eden put his hand up on her muzzle, and she became calmer, although her eyes still rolled with fear.

"Take her away at once!" said Sophie.

Hannah hesitated, ready to argue, and in that moment Gladly arched her back and tail.

"Out! Out!" Sophie bellowed.

"No, Gladly!" cried Hannah.

Too late. A waterfall hit the concrete floor and sprayed up over coats, boots, boxes of kindling wood, and the kitchen door. Mikey started to laugh. Eden, although he was being splashed, put his hand over his mouth and laughed, too.

"Move that animal!" shrieked Sophie.

But Gladly would not be moved until she had finished, by which time the porch floor was a frothing tide, and nearly everything in it was dripping.

Sophie was furious, but Mikey knew she wouldn't be able to say too much, not without making Eden feel bad. Eden was laughing so much he probably didn't notice Sophie's anger. He pointed to the splashes on his legs. "Went down my boots!"

Sky and Joe came running from the garage to see what the noise was about. In a moment they were laughing, too.

Sophie couldn't see the funny side. She barked at Hannah, "You've got some cleaning to do, young woman. No, not Eden. It was your idea. The floor, these coats, boots! Get some disinfectant and a scrubbing brush!"

Hannah was backing Gladly off the porch.

Mikey was amazed that a horse could have so much liquid in it. It was like a sea. "I'll help you," he said to Hannah.

"Me, too," said Eden.

"We'll all help," said Joe. "Hannah, while you're putting her back in her paddock, you might work out how you're going to fit this into one of your stories."

They took out the wet boots and coats and filled buckets with hot, soapy water.

Sky said, "Here's a joke. Where do sick horses go?"

"To the horse piddle!" said Eden, and they all started laughing again.

Joe had done some work on the car to get ready for the Christchurch trip, and he wanted to take it for a trial run. On Sunday morning, he put the snorkeling gear in the trunk and said, "Who wants to go to Titirangi Beach to get some paua?"

Mikey nearly didn't go. He still wasn't sure which locomotive he wanted, and he needed quiet space for decision making. In the end, he took the train catalog with him.

The road to Titirangi looked like an old cow path. It was steep, narrow, carved out of rock, and it had mountain beech forest on either side. Because this was Eden's first time on the road, Joe kept stopping to show him the view through the gaps in the bush—the distant deep blue of Endeavour Inlet, with houses and boats ant-size in the bays. It was a warm enough day, almost summer, but high up on the road near Mount Stokes, the air was cool with ragged clouds hanging in the trees like old fleece. Mikey thought this part of the road always looked like a movie set for a thriller. Hannah said it was a place of power, which was why she used it for her story.

"These are the trees that walk at night," she said. "See how old they are? Look at the moss and lichen growing on their bodies. Look at the orchids and ferns like sleeves on their arms."

Eden wound down his window and put his head out.

"Behold," said Hannah. "The forest of Raku and Drakmar."

"Stop!" said Eden.

As Joe slowed the car, Sophie turned in her seat, "Do you want to get out, Eden? All right. Joe, give us a few minutes. I wouldn't mind getting some lichen to dye wool."

"Don't be too long," said Joe. "We don't want to miss low tide at Titirangi."

Mikey stayed in the car, looking at his catalog. Joe walked down the road with his hands in his pockets, whistling, stopping every now and then to look out at the sea. The others climbed up the steep bank on the other side of the road and disappeared into the beech forest. They didn't go far. Mikey could see Sky near the bank, reaching out to pull a tuft of lichen from a black tree trunk. He heard Hannah's voice floating down like a long, thin banner, "This is the place where Raku overcame the lord of the trolls to rescue Drakmar from a life of slavery in the troll's mountain mine. Here are the branches broken in their struggle…"

Mikey made up his mind. He would buy the miniature of the Flying Scotsman steam engine, which had run between London and Edinburgh. It was expensive, but being just about the most famous engine in the world, it would make a good beginning to his collection.

He showed the picture to Joe, who said, "Good choice."

"It costs a lot."

Joe replied, "If it's what you want, get it, because once you've set your mind on it you won't be happy with anything else."

That was true. Mikey said, "We are definitely going on Tuesday? You won't change your mind?"

Joe smiled. "It'd be more than my life is worth."

The others came down the bank with twigs in their clothes and hair and a lumpy plastic bag that filled the car with the rotten wood smell of lichen. Sky had scratched his knee on a rock and was squeezing the wound, trying to enlarge a drop of blood, which sat like a ruby on his skin. Sky liked blood. Once he had painted a picture with a cut finger. Now he chanted, "We've got skin to keep us in, but when our skin gets a leak...Hey! What rhymes with leak?"

"Squeak?" suggested Sophie. "Peek? Streak?"

"How about—we get weak?" said Joe.

"Those are the flowers!" exclaimed Hannah, pointing to tufts of white daisies at the edge of the road. "The flowers of lightness which Drakmar eats so he can fly. They don't bloom all year. Only early summer. In winter, Drakmar runs beside Raku and Sassenach. In summer he flies over their heads, turning his body to glide in and out of trees."

Mikey rolled up his frayed catalog. "Let's talk about something interesting."

"Like trains?" said Sophie.

"Like food," Mikey said.

"The sandwiches are in the trunk of the car," said Joe. "I'm not stopping again. But here's a snack." He pulled a bag of candy from the shelf under the dashboard. "Help yourself."

They handed the bag around, but even a mouth full of candy did not stop Hannah. "Here is where Drakmar can leap and swoop right down to the water's edge."

"Like a bungee jump without a cord," said Sky.

"More like a gannet flying. Down, straight into the water with his hands out in front of him to catch a snapper. Then he goes back to cook it on a forest fire."

"Come off it, Han," said Mikey. "How can anyone catch a snapper with bare hands? What about the spines?"

Eden turned. "You don't know everything!"

"I know about two thousand percent more than you!" Mikey retorted.

"That's enough, Mikey!" said Sophie. "Not another word!"

He sat back and folded his arms. "Edenitis," he said to himself. Edenitis, Weedenitis. It just wasn't fair!

Down in Titirangi Bay, they parked the car in the campground and walked through the sandhills to the beach. The sea was calm right out to the islands, which shimmered on the horizon. The edge of the water could hardly be called a wave. It simply turned over, collapsed on the sand with a sigh, and then went out again, raking empty shells and crab claws.

Sophie took her bucket into the shallows to

get some tuatua. Hannah, Eden, and Sky went with her. Hannah showed Eden how to dig through the sand for the white, oval shells, and Mikey guessed from the hum of her voice and the way the three heads were together that the story was continuing.

He went with Joe to the end of the beach where they usually got the paua. In this place the sand turned to rocks covered with shining seaweed and clumps of blue mussels. Joe put down the snorkeling gear, and Mikey found a potato sack with ties on it, which he fastened around his waist like an apron. With a blunt knife in one hand and his mask and snorkel in the other, he waded into the water. The sea was icy cold! Every step, he had to stand still to get used to the new depth. The worst was when the water reached his stomach. He gasped and rinsed out his mask. Then, wiping his hair away from his forehead, he set the mask and snorkel firmly in place.

Joe was one of those people who ran and crashed into the water whatever its temperature. He was already kicking along the line of rocks, looking for paua.

Mikey quietly lowered the rest of himself into the water. As his face broke the skin of the sea, he entered its world. It was like another universe, silent except for the murmuring of water against his ears and the sound of his breathing.

Today there was no swell to stir up the sand, and the water was so clear that he could see ahead to the forests of brown kelp that waved slowly back and forth. Between the clumps of kelp were patches of sand rippling in the sunlight. The water was about three feet deep, too shallow for bigger fish, but he saw spotties, like little patched ghosts, and a shoal of herring on the move, glinting silver.

He wasn't wearing fins. His kick was slow and free. He moved into the kelp and parted the brown fronds. There were several undersized paua here, cupped against the rocks. Kina, too. Joe was crazy about those prickly sea urchins, and he would probably have picked up half a sack by now. Mikey did not bother. Their spines were sharp, and they usually came through the sack to prick his legs while he was swimming.

His body had become accustomed to the cold, and now he could feel the sun on his back. The water against his skin was soft and slippery like the satin sheets Aunt Katie had bought Joe and Sophie for Christmas. He swam farther out, parting the seaweed, watching the crevices in the rocks. Red-eyed sea anemones blinked like traffic lights. There were yellow sponges and long stemmed barnacles and large cat's eye snails—pupu, Joe called them. He came across a large paddle crab half buried in the sand. It would have been good for eating, but it was waving its claws at him, and he didn't want to pick it up without diving gloves. Those claws could nip through the skin like scissors.

And there was a big paua!

He dived, holding onto the kelp with one hand while he thrust his knife between the paua and the rock. The paua came off and rolled away. He saw its underside, black in a blue rim of shell, and then it disappeared into a rocky crevice. He went down after it, his ears drumming. His breath was running out. Down, down, he went, groping between the rocks. He had it! He shot up to the surface, blowing like a whale, and rolled onto his back to put the paua in his bag. Yes, it was a good one.

He found four more farther away, but now he was feeling the cold again, not on his skin but deep in his bones. He put his head up and heard a noise. Joe was on the beach, calling, beckoning.

It took him a long time to get back. His bones seemed to be made of ice, and his movements were slow and clumsy. As he walked through the shallows, Joe said, "You're blue!"

His jaw was stiff as he said, "I got five good paua."

"I've got three and some kina. Do you have a towel?"

"No."

"Use mine. We'll go straight back to the car.

You look frozen."

"I'm all right." But he didn't feel all right. The cold inside his body was so intense that the outside didn't want to move.

They went back to the campground. Mikey changed into dry clothes while Joe lit a fire in one of the fireplaces. He heaped driftwood and pine cones on it and told Mikey to sit close. Mikey did, but his bones remained cold. Now he was shivering with big earthquake shivers.

The others came up the beach with a bucket half full of tuatua. "Fritters," said Sophie. "Clam chowder. Mikey, you look cold. Where's your sweater?"

"He didn't bring it," said Joe.

"Silly fool. You can have mine," said Sophie. She was about to pull her brown homespun over her head when Eden came from the car, holding out his quilted windbreaker.

"Thanks, Eden," said Sophie. "That'll do nicely."

Mikey's teeth were chattering a frantic Morse code, but he turned away. "I'll be all right."

"Put it on."

"It's too small."

"Nah," said Eden. "It's big on me. Ginormous."

Joe said, "Mikey, you have hypothermia. Put Eden's jacket on, and stop fooling around."

Mikey saw it in front of him, pink and green with fancy studs and zippers, hanging from Eden's outstretched hand. He stood up. "I told you I'm okay!" he shouted as he walked away.

CHAPTER TEN

On Tuesday, when Hannah came home from school, she found that Sophie had been dyeing spun wool with different kinds of lichen in pots on the stove. Hanks of yellow, orange, and mauve hung dripping from the clothesline.

"I'm finished!" said Sophie, taking off her apron. "Are you taking Gladly out? Good. Mind if I come, too?"

Hannah could not remember when they had last taken a walk without the rest of the family. When they were all together, the talk tended to be of things outside of themselves. There was usually a noisy trading of information, jokes, puzzles, songs, stories. On those rare times when Sophie and Hannah talked on their own, the world seemed to shrink to the size of two people's feelings. Hannah liked the way Sophie listened and asked her opinions about things.

Sophie didn't always have the answers to Hannah's questions. Sometimes she said, "I don't know," and that made Hannah feel good, too.

They went for a long walk over the hills, leading Gladly some of the time, at others letting her follow with her rope trailing. Hannah kept giving her pieces of bread while she and Sophie discussed how they felt about high school, growing up, bikinis, netball versus football, and boyfriends.

"Boyfriends?" cried Hannah. "No way!"

"Tell me about it in another three years," said Sophie.

Hannah shook her head. "I'll be too busy for that stuff. Yuck!"

"Yuck can change when you meet someone you like," Sophie replied.

"Is that how it was when you met Joe?"

"Oh, long before your father. I must have been in love half a dozen times."

"Then how could you be sure about him?"

"With Joe it was more than just falling in love. He was my best friend. It's friendship that makes a relationship permanent."

Hannah said, "I think friendship is the most important thing in the world."

"It is," said Sophie. She smiled. "Look at us now. Isn't it nice to be free of the mother and daughter role, to talk as friends?"

"We should do it more often," Hannah said.

They both turned to see if Gladly was still following.

"The parent role can be kind of a trap," said Sophie. "Mothers and fathers are expected to talk to children in a certain way. Certain responses are expected from the children. It's as though someone had written a script for the parts. Joe and I thought we'd break away from that by having you call us by our first names. But we still do it. If I'm not careful, I start quoting the script instead of being me. On Saturday, when Gladly did that monstrous pee on the porch, I was dying to laugh. But I couldn't because I had to be the mother."

"I thought you were really angry," said Hannah.

Sophie hesitated, "Maybe I was to begin with…"

"But you couldn't say too much without making Eden feel guilty about wetting the bed."

Sophie laughed. "Hannah! The bed doesn't matter. Eden doesn't do a bucketful!"

They stopped and fed Gladly another piece of bread. Sophie stopped laughing, was quiet for a moment, then said, "The other day I heard you tell Mikey he was jealous."

"He is."

"That's why it shouldn't be said. Jealousy is a very demanding emotion, and being Mikey, he'll feel burdened by it. It's been hard for both the boys."

"Sky's all right."

"Not really. He reveals it in other ways, by showing off a lot and demanding extra attention. He's been coming into our bed nearly every night lately, complaining of bad dreams."

Hannah tried to read her mother's face. "Sophie, you aren't going to send Eden back, are you?"

"No. We can't unless something really awful happens. In spite of everything, he actually likes it here. He likes the animals. He feels useful. He's adjusting much faster than I thought he would. What I didn't anticipate was the effect on the family, especially Mikey. I always thought Mikey was so solid and easygoing."

"He hates Eden," said Hannah.

"I don't know about hate. He certainly doesn't like him."

"Eden does try to be nice to him—sometimes. That seems to make Mikey worse."

Sophie said, "Poor Eden. He was terribly afraid he was going back today. He wouldn't believe us until he actually got in the car and saw that his clothes hadn't been packed. And you know? Last night, for the first time, he hugged me. It wasn't much of a hug. He leaned against me for a second and then took off. But it made me think of Saint-Exupéry's book *The Little Prince*. In there it says that when you tame something, you are responsible for it for the rest of its life."

They began to walk back toward the horse paddock.

Sophie said, "How do you feel about him spending so much time with Gladly?"

"I don't mind. Gladly is my horse. He knows that. So does Gladly. I don't care if he goes up there and talks to her. She needs a lot of handling."

"Will you let him ride her while you're away at high school?"

"Sophie, he won't be able to. Mrs. Gerritsen will break her, but Gladly's still going to be very high-spirited. It's her nature. Eden's never ridden a horse in his life. He's small. He couldn't control her. She'll throw him, and he could get hurt."

"She's actually very quiet with him," Sophie said.

"Riding is different. You don't give a horse like this to a beginner." She picked up Gladly's rope. "He can learn to ride on another horse. Debbie's pony is quiet. But he can't ride Gladly until he's had a lot of experience."

"You wouldn't mind?"

"Not if he knew what he was doing." Hannah felt herself getting angry. She changed the subject. "What are you going to do about Mikey?"

"I don't know."

"He can sleep in my room if he wants to. It's only another three months and I'll be at boarding school."

"Thanks," said Sophie. "I'll remember that. Do you want to do me a favor, Hannah? Spend a moment or two thinking about the amount of time you used to spend with Mikey before Eden came on the scene."

"What do you mean by that?" Hannah said sharply.

"It's not a judgment," said Sophie. "It's a request." She smiled at Hannah. "We'll see how he is with his new train. That might do a lot for him."

That night they boiled tuatua, shelled them, and made a thick clam chowder. Because the others would be late getting back from Christchurch, they ate their chowder early and left the rest in the pot. For dessert, they dribbled strawberry jam over homemade ice cream. Then Hannah helped Sophie wind the hanks of dyed wool into balls ready for knitting.

They heard the car sometime after nine. Mikey came in first like Santa Claus, laden with plastic shopping bags. He greeted Hannah and Sophie, but there was something strange about his smile and the way he hurried through the door toward his bedroom.

Sky was his usual self. He burst in to hug Sophie and show them a pack of pink and white candy shaped like false teeth, which he had bought with his allowance.

Joe and Eden were last, and the energy they dragged through the back door was so bad you could almost smell it. Joe was tired. He had a heavy look. Eden was pale from carsickness, but at the same time his face was screwed up in a knot of fury. "He has my knife!" he spat at Sophie, as he went toward the bathroom.

Joe let out a breath that seemed to come from the bottom of his feet. He put down on the table a red Swiss army knife and said, "This fell out of his pocket."

"Where did he get it?" asked Sophie.

Joe shook his head. "We went back to the train and hobby shop. It didn't come from there. I tried a couple of other places…"

"Joe…"

"I know, I know. But I don't have eyes in the back of my head. After we'd been to the Social Welfare office, we met Mikey. He wanted me to look at some trains. Eden got bored and wandered off."

Hannah turned up the heat under the clam chowder. She saw Sophie's face fill up with tiredness and become like Joe's, and she felt angry with Eden. The stupid kid! What a rotten, dumb thing to do!

"It dropped out of his pocket when he was getting into the car," said Joe.

"What was his explanation?" Sophie asked.

Joe gave her a dry, humorless smile. "He says the Godsiffs gave it to him."

"What?"

"He repeats it like a parrot. They gave it to him last Friday night."

"Oh, no!" Sophie went toward the phone. "Here we go again."

"They're not at home," Joe said. "Away all week, remember? That's why he used them as an excuse. He knew we couldn't check it out." Joe spread his hands. "It was getting late. I couldn't go around to every store in the area asking if they had lost a Swiss army knife. I don't know what to do."

Hannah stirred the chowder. She said quietly, "I think he did take it from the Godsiffs. Glen has a knife like that. Maybe Eden thought, well, he didn't get into too much trouble over Debbie's game. Maybe…"

"He thought this time he'd get away with it," said Joe.

"They were so nice," said Sophie. "Inviting him to dinner and doing their best…" She stopped, for Eden was coming back into the room.

He saw the knife on the table and tried to snatch it, but Joe got it first.

"That's my knife!" Eden cried. "Give it to me!'
He struggled to unlock Joe's hand. "It's mine!
Mine!"

"That's enough, Eden," said Sophie.

The boy stopped and began to cry, "He stole
it from me!" he said to Sophie. "He's a thief!"
Then he ran out of the room, slamming the door.

CHAPTER ELEVEN

Mikey let Sky help him assemble the track on the sitting room table. He had wanted to do it on his own, fearing that if he allowed Sky in, he would have to have Eden, too. But Eden had taken Gladly for a walk, and was nowhere near.

"You can put some of the track together, but don't touch the wiring," he said to Sky.

The table had belonged to Sophie's grandmother and mother. It was a farmhouse kitchen table, made of kauri and over nine feet long, with thick, turned legs. Too big for this family's kitchen, it had been put in the front room for Sophie's table loom and her baskets of wool. It could hold a large figure eight of track with space to spare.

"Can I unpack the engine?" Sky asked.

"No, I'll do that. You get the cars ready."

The black locomotive was a perfect miniature of the London-to-Edinburgh Flying Scotsman. It had solid wheels and pistons and an open cab that showed a tiny firebox and brake. Mikey breathed softly over it.

Sky pushed his head in. "Where's the steering wheel?"

That made Mikey laugh. "You nut!"

"Why nut?"

"The train's steering wheel is its track."

"Oh. Oh, yeah." Sky did a dance round the table. "A track is a thing that a train runs on. Yeah, yeah, ziggy-bob yeah."

"Where do you get this ziggy-bob business from?" Mikey asked as he connected the engine to the cars.

"From Ziggy-bob"

"What's that?"

"Not what. Who. It's my secret name."

Mikey laughed. "You're as bad as Hannah, the way you make up things. Why secret?"

"Well, I like changing my name, but it confuses people. So I change it secretly and say it in disguise. Ziggy-bob, yeah!"

Mikey was connecting the extension cord to the lead from the transformer. He pushed the plug into the outlet. The transformer hummed, and a red light went on.

"It's going!" Sky shouted.

"Don't sound so surprised." Mickey checked the rail connections and put his head against the table to make sure all the wheels were gripping the track. "Ready?" he said.

Sky nodded.

Mikey turned the switch on the transformer.

The locomotive's light went on, the wheels turned with a real train noise, and the engine ran along the track, hauling two cars and a caboose. The tiny pistons on the engine went faster than the eye could see, and the crankshafts pumped like busy arms. Mikey varied the speed. Too fast—the wheels left the track on the curve, and the engine fell over, taking the cars with it. He set them up again and changed the train's course from the outside oval to the inner figure eight and back again. He put Sophie's book *The Woolcrafter's Guide* upside down and open over the track to make a tunnel.

Sky went out and called Joe and Sophie to come and look. Hannah came, too. She admired the train while Sophie reminded everyone that breakfast was ready and they had only fifteen minutes until the school bus arrived.

"You need a real tunnel," said Joe. "It's easy to make one with papier-mâché and chicken wire."

"That's not all I need. A real layout! Another train! More track! You see why I had to extend my eeling business?"

"You'll need a train to take you to school if you don't hurry," said Sophie. "Where's Eden?"

"He's out with Gladly," said Sky. "I saw them on the beach."

"Beach?" cried Hannah. "You're sure?"

"Yep." Sky pulled back the curtain from the front window. "Take a look."

"I told him the woolshed and no farther!" said Hannah. "See? See over there? He's taken her into the water!"

Sophie said, "Sky, run down and tell Eden to bring Gladly right back. Tell him it's late."

"Gladly's in the sea!" Hannah cried.

Joe and Mikey stood beside her. Eden was walking parallel to the shore and up to his knees in water, holding Gladly's rope. She was splashing after him, lifting her hooves high as though in some dressage exercise.

Hannah was close to tears. "She doesn't like the water! How could he do that! Only to the woolshed, I told him!"

Joe said, "Right now, Eden's angry with everyone—except Gladly."

"She isn't his horse!" Hannah said.

"Well," said Joe. "He hasn't done her any harm. If I were you, Hannah, I'd let it pass. We have the pocketknife to deal with, and that's enough for the moment." He turned and gave Mikey a warning look. "Don't mention the knife to anyone at school. No one, do you hear? We'll wait until the Godsiffs get back."

"It is Glen's," said Hannah. "I'm sure about that."

"Then it's no one else's business," said Joe.

Mikey shrugged. He thought that if someone in the class went around burgling desks and bags and stealing things when they were invited to dinner, then everyone should know about it.

He looked at his father's face, grim with worry, and closed his mind on sympathy. It was their own fault. He had warned them, hadn't he? And now it was only a matter of time.

At school he had his train to talk about. Some of his friends wanted to bike down that afternoon to see it. He told them to wait until Saturday, and then maybe they could help him make some hills and a tunnel.

"How big are you going to build it?" someone asked.

Mikey shrugged. "I haven't decided yet. But I'll tell you this, the more eels you catch, the quicker it will grow."

He and Sky played with the train again after school. They searched through old toys looking for small cars and trucks to set up at intersections, and they made a station from a cereal box. It was all rough, with nothing to scale, but that didn't matter right now. Hannah reckoned she could help Mikey build a truss bridge. Sophie thought that lichen glued on twigs would make realistic trees.

While they were discussing layout, Eden came up and stood in the doorway. He didn't enter the room, just stood there for a few seconds and then went outside.

Later, Mikey told Sky to close the door.

Joe cooked paua steaks that night. Because Eden didn't like shellfish, Joe fried him a couple of sausages. The food was ready to go on the table, but Eden wasn't in the house.

Sophie said, "He'll be in the horse paddock. Mikey, go and get him."

"Why can't Hannah go?"

"Mikey!" sighed Sophie.

"I don't have to! Tell Hannah—or Sky!"

Joe said, "Mikey! Up with this I will not put!" He tried to make a joke of it, but his voice was like stretched elastic.

Mikey scraped his chair back across the floor and stamped out to the porch to put on his boots. It's not fair, he said to himself. This had nothing to do with him.

He went through the back gate, kicking at a plastic bucket that had been lying by the garden faucet. The noise made some sheep turn and trot away across the slope.

It was all their idea. If the Weed wouldn't come in for his supper, they should handle the problem.

Hannah came out after him. He was walking up the hill to the horse paddock when he heard the slop slop of her boots. He saw her running toward him, her hair flying. He looked away.

"Wait for me!" she yelled.

He walked slowly. The days were long now and felt like summer. The sun was warm between the shadows, and the air was full of insects that rose and fell like specks of golden dust. Out in the bay, the water was flat except for pools near the shore where herring jumped. The splashes glinted silver like the wheels of his train.

"Mikey?"

He stopped. The sun shone through her hair. It looked as though it was on fire. She caught up with him, and they walked without speaking to the paddock. It felt good to have her with him.

At first they saw only Gladly. She was way up the hill near the bush, and she was grazing. She walked slowly from one clump to another, without lifting her head.

Then they saw Eden. He was on Gladly's back, lying across her mane.

Hannah made a high-pitched noise through her nose but didn't say anything.

Mikey called, "Eden? Supper's ready! You've got to come right now!"

Eden slid off Gladly's back and came down the hill. The filly went on eating.

Hannah was breathing fast. As Eden came near, she yelled, "You leave her alone!"

Eden stopped, stared at her, and changed direction. He walked away from them, climbed over the fence, and then went toward the house.

Hannah ran after him. "You think you're smart!" Her voice was shrill with fury. "Just because people feel sorry for you, you take advantage! You steal everything!"

He looked at her over his shoulder.

"You're not having her!" she screamed. "Got that? Don't you ever go near Gladly again!"

CHAPTER TWELVE

Hannah dreamed that Eden rode Gladly through the school grounds and into the classroom. He was dressed in a storybook soldier's uniform, red with gold braid, and a high hat with a peak. Gladly clop-clopped across the wooden boards to Hannah's desk, and Hannah heard herself shout at Eden, "Get down! This is my horse, and you can't have her!" In the dream Eden laughed at her. And then she saw that he had no legs. He was a centaur—a mythological creature half boy and half horse. Eden was actually Gladly. A cry of pain swelled in Hannah's chest and came up to her throat, where it stuck. She woke up, gasping for air, her heart pounding.

She didn't know what time it was. A half-moon silvered the top part of her window and showed the outlines of her bedroom furniture.

The familiar things did not comfort her. The sadness from her dream remained and became real. She had gone through the grief of Shadrach's death, and then, miraculously, Gladly had happened. Shadrach's daughter. It had been a miracle, Shadrach returning half of himself to her.

Now she was losing Gladly. The awful thing about it was that Eden wasn't really taking the filly away from Hannah. Gladly was choosing him. She preferred Eden's company.

Hannah turned her face into her pillow, trying to erase last night's memory of Eden on Gladly's back. He must have hypnotized her. How else could he have gotten on a horse that hadn't been broken? She was nearly seventeen hands and a wild thing. He was little and didn't know anything about riding. If Hannah had not seen it for herself, she would not have believed Mikey in a thousand years.

Last night she had been hurting too much to continue the Raku and Drakmar serial. The story had gotten to the stage where Raku had found the spring of life, and she and Drakmar were trying to take some water back to the rimu giant who was dying of a chain saw cut.

"Just tell us if he died or not," pleaded Sky.

She shook her head.

"Please, Hannah-banner!"

Eden had his eyes closed, pretending to sleep.

"No, I don't feel like it."

"You're mean!" Sky had said, "Mean, mean, moldy old bean."

Hannah punched her pillow to soften it and pulled the covers around her neck. She tried chanting her sleep-making poem, two lines from Alfred, Lord Tennyson's "The Lotos-Eaters:"

Music that gentlier on the spirit lies,
Than tired eyelids upon tired eyes.

That usually made her feel drowsy but not tonight. She kept hearing the sound of Gladly's hooves and seeing Eden's smile in her dream. She thought that she would have to lie awake until morning, but she must have dozed. The next time she opened her eyes, there was a square of sunlight on her bed, and she could hear Mikey and Sky talking in the living room.

She kicked back the covers, got up, and went down the hall. Her brothers were still in their pajamas, watching the train rattle around the track. Hannah yawned and stretched her arms above her head.

Mikey looked at her. "I think Eden's with Gladly again."

Her arms dropped to her sides.

Sky said, "He wasn't in bed when we woke up. He must have gotten up real early."

"So you wouldn't catch him, I suppose," said Mikey.

Hannah ran to her bedroom to pull on her clothes. She was full of anger, which made her clumsy. The zipper on her jeans got stuck, and her sweater went on inside out. She ran through the kitchen and to the porch for her boots.

The paddock was empty, the gate open. She went farther up the slope to a place where she could see most of the farm and the bay in front of it. The land was soft under early morning shadow, and the air was clear, smelling of animals and earth and wet grass. There was no sign of Eden or the horse.

Sophie was not all that helpful. Half-asleep and concerned with breakfast and school lunches, she mumbled things like, "He's just taken her for a walk" and "They'll be back soon."

"I told you they're not anywhere in the bay!"

"Yes, Dear. Will you keep an eye on that toast?"

"I looked all over the farm and down on the beach."

"I'm sure I put another loaf out to defrost. Hannah, is there a loaf of bread on that end of the counter?"

"I told him not to go near Gladly again!"

"Wasn't that being a bit high-handed?"

"She is my horse, Sophie. I decide what is

best for her. But he ignored me. He just took her without asking."

"I suppose there wasn't much point in asking when you were going to say no. Where did I put that bread? You told him he could help exercise her."

"That was before last night. You didn't see…"

"Hannah! The toast! It's burning!"

An hour later, Eden had not returned. They all went out on the farm to look for him. Joe was worried.

"A big, high-spirited filly like that shouldn't be with an inexperienced child. Last night he might have climbed on her back when she was in a quiet mood. This morning she could have tossed him to the wind."

He backed the car out and searched along the road and beach in both directions. Sky and Mikey went with Sophie over the top hill and into the bush. Hannah looked along the track by the stream.

Then the children ran out of time and had to go back to the house to get ready for school.

"I'll bring your lunches to you," said Sophie. "Got your homework? Hurry up or you'll miss the bus."

That was when they discovered that Eden's school bag was missing.

There wasn't time for more. Mrs. Gerritsen was honking at the gate, and the next minute they were running down the driveway, organizing jackets, books, and bags as they went.

"No Eden this morning?" Mrs. Gerritsen asked.

Hannah shook her head and then, because Mrs. Gerritsen was still looking a question at her, she added, "Sophie will probably bring him to school at lunchtime."

When the lunch hour came, Sophie walked into the school with their lunch boxes, but there was no Eden.

Sophie said to Hannah, "The comforter is gone from his bed."

"You think he took it with him?"

"I don't know where else it could be. His school bag's gone, too. I haven't been able to find a loaf of bread, a jar of raspberry jam, and those chocolate chip cookies Mikey made."

"So he ran away."

"It looks like it."

Then the enormity of it hit Hannah. "He's taken Gladly! He's stolen her!"

"Hannah…"

"He can't take Gladly!"

Sophie said, "I think he plans to hide out somewhere."

"No one can hide a horse that big!"

Sophie smiled through her anxiety. "I seem to remember some children who ran away from home and hid a large horse in a school, a camper, and a barge. It's funny how history repeats itself."

"That was different!" said Hannah. "We were saving Shadrach from the dog food factory!"

Sophie shut her eyes for a second. "Maybe Eden is trying to save himself."

"Why did he steal Gladly?"

"He didn't steal her. He just took her with him—for company, I suppose."

"So what's the difference?"

Sophie shook her head. "Hannah, this is not very helpful. Joe and I have combed the area. Up and down this road, every hay barn, every woolshed, the Godsiffs' house. We've had a terrible morning. Joe still believes he's lying somewhere unconscious or worse."

Hannah put her arm around her mother's shoulder. "Sorry, Sophie. What'll you do now?"

Sophie gave her a quick absent-minded kiss on the cheek. "I'm going to have a talk with Mr. Gerritsen, and then I'm going to call the police."

CHAPTER THIRTEEN

Mikey didn't have a chance to look at his train that afternoon. When he got home from school, a police car was in the driveway, and Sergeant Duff was talking to Joe and Sophie at the kitchen table. Mikey knew the sergeant. He had once been to the school to talk about keeping yourself safe. He was about Joe's age but with fair skin, reddish hair, and a wide, floppy mouth that filled up his face when he smiled. He smiled a lot, but he also had quick eyes that saw everything. Even while he was drinking coffee and talking, he was sizing up the room.

He asked them a lot of questions about Eden, especially about last night, and Mikey felt sorry for Hannah having to describe what happened in the horse paddock. Sergeant Duff had the habit of repeating those parts that were hardest to tell.

"You didn't like him being close to your horse."

"I didn't mind—I—" Hannah looked away. "No."

"And you told him not to go near her again?"

"Yes."

He asked Mikey the same difficult questions. Did he get along well with Eden? What did they talk about yesterday? The big mouth smiled, but above it, the eyes bored right through Mikey's eyes and into his brain.

"So you really don't get along with him at all."

"I don't like the way he…"

"Oh, Mikey!" Sophie said.

"He steals things! He tells lies all the time!"

Sergeant Duff's smile got wider. "When I was a little kid I sometimes stole things and told lies. Children will do that sort of thing."

"He's not our family!" Mikey cried. "He doesn't belong here!" There was a bit of a silence; then he mumbled, "Can I go now? I have to look at my eel trap."

Hannah said to the sergeant, "What if Eden tries to get back at us? What if he hurts Gladly?"

He shook his head. "I don't think so. The horse is his friend. If you ask me, Eden ran away because he thought you were going to send him back to Christchurch. He won't be far from here. We'll find him. I want you to think carefully. Is there something you haven't told me? It doesn't matter how unimportant you think it is. Perhaps he talked about a place."

"The forest of Raku and Drakmar!" said Sky.

"It's the beech forest up Mount Stokes," Hannah explained. "We made up a story about it."

"We looked there this afternoon," said Sophie.

"We'll look again," said Sergeant Duff. "Sometimes children get scared of the consequences of being found. They hide from searchers. You can pass within a foot of them and not know they're there. Did you name any particular spot in these stories?"

Hannah shook her head. "Not real names." Then she said, "There is something—although it might be nothing. Last night I had a dream. It was about Eden and Gladly, and the noise woke me up. It could have been real."

"What noise?"

"Horse's hooves. You know how you dream the phone is ringing, and you wake up and it is? It was like that. I heard a clop-clopping noise, but afterward, when I was really awake, there was nothing."

Joe said to the sergeant, "Hannah's window faces the driveway."

"What time was this?" Sergeant Duff asked.

"I don't know. I didn't turn on the light. The moon was shining, but it wasn't bright enough…"

"Moon? Could you see it?"

"Yes, it was showing in the top of the window."

"Can you show me where in the window? Let me see your room. We might be able to work out the time from the moon's position."

Sky nudged Hannah, "Wow!" he whispered. "He's doing real detective stuff."

Mikey was kicking the table. "Can I go now?" he repeated.

Chapter Fourteen

Mikey pedaled toward the river with his sack and a container of possum meat bait. His wheels spun over clay and stones, and the wet smell of the bush closed around him. Joe said the bush always got this damp smell before rain. Mikey looked up at the sky, where clouds were heaping up like dirty fleeces on the woolshed floor. He wondered what would happen if they didn't find Eden tonight. He was such a spindly little kid.

He looked for signs along the road, hoof marks, a movement in the trees. The green umbrellas of ferns passed over his head, and the tall kanukas leaned out, their branches topped with the first white flowers of summer blooming. The bush was simply itself and hiding nothing. The squeak in his bike pedal formed the words, "not here, not here, not here."

At the head of the sound he left his bike by the fence, climbed over, and walked along the riverbank. He was sure that Sergeant Duff thought it was all his fault. But it wasn't! Right from the beginning he had told his family that they'd regret it, and they had only given him their pained "Oh, Mikey!" look. He wasn't jealous. He had just been trying to make them see the obvious.

As he walked, he continued to look, although he was sure he would not find anything here. For that matter, he didn't know what he was looking for. A boy with a horse? A horse on its own? Someone lying dead under a tree?

He blinked and shook his head. He was getting as bad as Hannah.

He had put the trap in a new place in the river by the pine plantation. As he had supposed, there were plenty of eels. The trap was so heavy that at first he thought it had moved under some submerged branches and got stuck. Then it sluggishly responded, and he knew it was full. He braced himself against a tree and pulled, hand over hand, winding the rope around a stump to prevent it from slipping back. When he got the basket over the bank, he saw that it had only four eels in it, but they were all big. The possum bait had been reduced to bone.

Drops of rain had begun to fall, heavy and widely spaced. Mikey looked at the sky. In a few moments there would be a downpour. He·gaffed one of the eels and hooked it out of the trap. His old jacket was no longer waterproof. He would get soaked on the way home. Then he thought of Eden, and he became angry. People would be out in the rain searching for the Weed. What did he think he was doing? Someone should give him a good talking to and straighten him out.

By the time all four eels were in the sack and the trap baited and reset, everything appeared to be under water. The cloud was down to the tops of the pine trees, and the rain was so thick it was almost solid. Mikey was soaked to the skin.

He half carried and half dragged the writhing sack to the road and clipped it to the carrier on his bike. The clay was now mud, and his wheels dragged in its wetness, spattering his boots and jeans with a yellowish-brown muck. He stood on his pedals, shaking his head to fling off the drops of water that ran from his hair and into his eyes. Even so, he couldn't see far. Straight lines of rain were like pencil scribble over the road.

Then he saw Gladly. She was in Webb's front paddock, and by the gate were two trucks. One was the yellow roadwork truck with Mr. Smith leaning out the window. The other belonged to Mr. and Mrs. Webb.

Gladly was trotting around the paddock, stopping every now and then to sniff at the grass. She wasn't wearing her halter, and her coat was dark with water.

Mikey got off his bike.

"We phoned your parents," Mr. Webb called. "There's no hurry to come and get the horse. She'll be all right here until tomorrow."

Mr. Smith got out of his truck. The rain was streaming off his yellow raincoat and rain pants. He grabbed Mikey's eel sack and then his bike and heaved them onto the bed of his truck. "Get in."

"Where's Eden?" Mikey asked.

"We don't know. I found the horse wandering on the road near Arran Craig's place. I think it's been on its own for a while. Get in before you drown."

"I'm too wet," said Mikey. "I'll sit on the back."

"That won't keep you from drowning. I'm wet, too. Hop inside."

Mikey opened the door and squelched up onto the seat. The windshield wipers were going at top speed, and a blast of hot air came from the heater in the cab.

"I'll take you home and then go back," Mr. Smith said. "The rest of the search party is up in the Titirangi Road area." He looked at Mikey. "Cheer up. We'll find him before dark."

Mikey didn't say anything. In spite of the warm air, he was feeling very cold. He wiped the wetness on his face with an even wetter sleeve and wished that this was yesterday, or maybe even last Sunday when he was shivering by the fire at Titirangi, and Eden was holding out his pink and green quilted jacket.

CHAPTER FIFTEEN

The next day they brought in a professional search and rescue team to direct the local operation. There were four men with search dogs and a helicopter that came and went from the parking lot near the school.

The noise invaded the classrooms—not only the chopper roaring but also trucks stopping and starting, dogs barking, people calling to each other. Even in the quieter moments, no one did much work. Hannah felt that in all the drama, Eden was more lost than ever. It was the helicopter that claimed everyone's attention. Each time it revved up, there would be a rush to the window to watch it take off and see who was in it. They all dreamed of having a ride.

The rain had stopped overnight, but the wind had turned to the south, and the temperature was cold enough for sweatshirts and thick socks. The weather worried them. Yesterday afternoon, when Mikey had come home like a drowned rat, Sophie had immediately run a hot bath for him. Hannah could tell that she was thinking of Eden in the way she yelled at Mikey to get his wet clothes off right away. Sophie wasn't the only one on edge. As pleased as Hannah was that Gladly had been found, she actually felt angry at the filly for being on her own.

Last night Sophie had given them pizza for supper. They sat around the table listening to the rain on the roof, aware of Eden's empty chair and that pizza was his favorite food. Obviously Sophie had believed he would be home.

When she woke up in the morning, Hannah thought that maybe Eden had come back in the night as quietly as he had disappeared. She didn't know why she had that idea. Maybe it was because she wanted it to happen. She got out of bed, turning her wish up to the strength of prayer, and went to the boys' room. Of course he wasn't there. Sky and Mikey were in their bunks, awake and talking. They stopped when they saw her.

"I thought you'd be with your train," she said to Mikey.

He shrugged and didn't reply.

"At least," she said, "they know which area he's in."

Joe got up extra early that morning to tend the animals before going to join the search party. He was blaming himself. "I overreacted when I found that knife. I shouldn't have gone on about it. I knew he was scared of us sending him back."

Sophie said, "Joe, Dear, you've just given the hens' food to the cat."

Twice Hannah had glimpsed Joe's red checkered shirt through the classroom window, and she wondered how Sophie was coping. It would be good if some of the neighbors were there, helping with the phone. There had been calls since daybreak. Eden's grandmother, who was Sophie's great aunt, had called to see if there was any news. So had other members of that family. Mrs. Parkes phoned several times, offering help. Then there were the people from the group home, a doctor Eden had seen, the search and rescue team, one of the dog handlers wanting to know if he could come for some of Eden's clothing to give the dogs the scent, and newspaper reporters asking for details of the story. No sooner would Sophie finish a call than the phone would ring again.

The helicopter was gone during the school lunch break, which was disappointing for those children who were still hoping for a free ride. Hannah was back in class and trying to concentrate on New Zealand history when some cars stopped and a group of people walked past the school. They were laughing and calling to someone.

Mr. Gerritsen saw them, too. "I think they've found him!" he said. "Just go on with your work. I'll find out." He went outside, and Hannah saw him running across the road. A moment later he was back. He held up his hand for silence. "No, Eden hasn't been found. But we do know that he's safe. They did another search of Mr. Craig's place, where Gladly was found. This time they took the dogs. They found an empty cookie tin and a quilt in a woodshed. There were also cookie crumbs. They think he slept in the shed last night."

"Where is he now?" someone asked.

"Not far away, we can be sure of that. The important thing is he's not hurt—and he had shelter from last night's rain."

Everyone was in a positive mood that afternoon. It would be only a matter of hours, they said, and the dogs would find him. He'd be home before dark, that was sure.

The helicopter left in the afternoon. There was nothing further it could do. The dogs were brought in, fed and watered, and then taken back by their handlers, who were also looking cheerful. "You'll have him in class with you tomorrow!" one called.

"Tomorrow's Saturday!" Sky shouted back.

When Hannah got home, she discovered that Gladly was in her own paddock, her head over the gate, snorting and whinnying for bread or apples. Hannah wanted to take her for a walk but couldn't. Sergeant Duff was at the house again, asking more questions.

"Hannah, I'm very interested in these stories you told Eden."

"She told me, too," said Sky.

"And Mikey as well, I suppose. Where is Mikey?"

Sky said, "He goes to his eel trap after school. No, he doesn't like stories all that much. He likes real things."

"And you know that Hannah's stories aren't real?"

"Of course."

"So does Eden," Hannah said.

"I'm glad you think so, Hannah. I don't have your talent for making up stories, but my wife and I do read books to our little girl. She's six. Often she doesn't know the difference between fact and fantasy. It's like that with television, too. We have to tell her what is real and what is made up."

"Eden is ten," Hannah said. "He's nearly Mikey's age."

The sergeant smiled his enormous smile. "Age is simply the number of years since we were born. It doesn't tell us how mature we are. A boy of ten might be twelve in some ways and only six or seven in others. From what we've been able to find out, Eden used to watch a lot of TV before he came here. That was real life as far as he was concerned. I'm wondering if he didn't think the same about your stories."

Hannah shook her head.

"Now, these stories were set in the Mount Stokes beech forest by the Titirangi Road, right?"

"Yes."

"And you think it's just a coincidence that Eden's in the same area?"

"He knew I made them up," Hannah said. "If he didn't like what was happening, he asked me to change it."

"I'd like to know more about these stories," the sergeant said.

"They're great!" said Sky. "Ziggy-bob cool!"

"Are there good guys and bad guys in them?"

Sky took over. "Drakmar and Raku are the good guys. They're brother and sister like me and Hannah, and the trees are their friends. Raku has a horse called Sassenach. The Doomroths are the bad guys."

"What are Doomroths?"

"They're like trolls," said Hannah. "They live under the earth."

"They hang their washing on the roots of trees," said Sky.

Sergeant Duff's smile grew so big that you could have driven a bus through it. He turned the page on his pad. "Start from the beginning, Hannah," he said.

Joe was late for dinner and so tired he could barely eat it. But he had to go out again, he said. "You wouldn't believe how much trash you can find in dense forest. How does it get there? Cigarette cartons, chocolate wrappers, bits of plastic, cartridge shells. Humanity is a dirty creation!" He looked at Mikey. "Anyone do another search of the woolshed?"

"And the henhouse and the garage," said Mikey.

"Everyone's been checking their own property," said Joe. "It has to be the forest area. But where? Thousands of acres, steep cliffs, rivers, beaches. I mean, he only has to get in the way of a wild boar..."

Sophie rubbed the back of his neck. "Joe, don't worry. Eden is a survivor."

"Yeah? Well, I sure don't think he survived very well here."

"Nobody made him go," said Hannah.

"Yeah," said Sky. "What did he run away for?"

"He probably thought we didn't like him," said Joe. "That would be a logical conclusion, wouldn't you say?"

"We do like him!" cried Hannah. "Just because I told him to leave Gladly alone doesn't mean…" She stopped and looked at Mikey.

"If anyone is interested," said Mikey. "I got five eels this afternoon."

Joe said, "I've been thinking about all the times I told him he was a part of the family. But that's not how we treated him. We made him feel like a guest who had stayed too long."

"I think I treated him like family," Sophie said.

"But he wasn't family, was he?" Mikey said bluntly. "He was different."

"Was?" said Sophie. "Don't you mean is?"

"We're all different," said Joe. "We like being different from each other. And we all get on each other's nerves from time to time. When Hannah gets in a dream world, she doesn't know what day it is. Mikey is the most stubborn creature this side of the planet Jupiter. Sky is noisy and can't sit still…"

"And he reads in the bathroom when the dishes are being done," said Hannah.

"Sophie and I? Sophie can get in a temper like an overturned beehive. I'm the source of all wisdom when it comes to giving advice but not so good at taking it."

"What is this?" said Sophie. "True confessions?"

"I'm just saying we are markedly different from each other and fairly tolerant of those differences. But we didn't accept the way Eden was different."

"I did," said Hannah.

"None of us did," said Joe. "We all wanted him to change. Adjust, we called it. We didn't like him as he was. You know what we did like? The idea of our own goodness. Wasn't it kind of us to give Eden a home…"

"Joe dear…" Sophie began.

"It was like getting a puppy from the pound. We were all over him for the first couple of weeks, and then the novelty began to wear off…"

"Joe?" Sophie put her arms around his neck and leaned over, her head against his. "They've probably found him by now."

"Mikey had a word for it," said Joe. "He called it 'Edenitis.' But Mikey had no right to criticize our giving when he himself was prepared to give nothing!"

"We all did what we thought was right," Sophie said.

"Heaven protect us from people who are convinced they are right," said Joe. "Do you know how much harm they cause the world?"

"Darling, you're very, very tired," said Sophie. "Why don't you have an early night?"

As Hannah watched them, she felt a tightness and then a pain invade her stomach. She knew why they were talking this way. They both thought that Eden was dead.

Joe put on his thick jacket, took two flashlights, and went out again. The boys went to the front room and the train. Hannah spread her homework over the kitchen table and tried to write about the Treaty of Waitangi while listening to her mother on the phone. The latest was a call from a woman in Blenheim who had set up a prayer chain for the missing child.

"I thanked her," Sophie told Hannah. "I said we needed all the help we could get."

They heard a car in the driveway, and both thought it was Joe. They stood up and opened the back door. It was Mrs. Godsiff.

"We just got home," she said. "I came as soon as I heard."

Sophie said, "How was the wedding?"

"Great! Nice catching up with everyone. When did he take off?"

"We think it was the early hours of yesterday morning," Sophie said. "It seems like weeks ago."

"What made him go?" Mrs. Godsiff asked.

"Who knows? Maybe a dozen things. He didn't give any kind of warning, but then being Eden, he wouldn't."

"I thought he was settling in really well," Mrs. Godsiff said. "He talked a lot last Friday. I heard him say something to Glen about his brothers. That's funny, I thought. I heard he was an only child."

"He invented things," said Sophie.

"So I asked him his brothers' names, and he looked at me as though I were the dumbest thing on earth and said, 'You know! Mikey and Sky!' I thought it was really nice."

Sophie's eyes closed for a moment.

"He's a great kid," Mrs. Godsiff said. "I'm just sorry we got off on the wrong foot over that silly game."

"Oh!" said Sophie. "It slipped my mind. Joe's got Glen's knife."

"Joe?"

"The Swiss army knife. I'm sorry. I should have mentioned it earlier."

"What about it?"

"Eden took it from your place," Sophie said.

"No he didn't. Glen gave it to him. That's Glen for you, feeling sorry because of the fuss over the game. I didn't know at the time or I would have told you."

"He really did give it to him?"

"It was no great sacrifice. He has two other knives. He said that Eden was tickled pink." Mrs. Godsiff stopped smiling. "You didn't accuse him of taking it, did you?"

Hannah didn't hear any more. She was running up the hall to the front room. She pushed open the door. "Guess what! That Swiss army knife did belong to Eden. Glen Godsiff gave it to him!"

"He did not!" said Mikey.

"Mrs. Godsiff said he did. She's in the kitchen right now. You can ask her."

Mikey looked at Hannah for a moment and then went back to the train.

"Come on!" Hannah insisted. "You come and ask!"

"Get off your high horse!" said Mikey.

After Mrs. Godsiff left and they were ready for bed, they went into the kitchen to say goodnight to Sophie.

Mikey said, "Hey Sophie, I've been thinking about this train layout."

"Mmmm," said Sophie, twisting a tissue between her fingers.

"You know how fussy Eden is—kind of neat about everything? Well, I thought he'd be good at making things to scale. Sophie, are you listening?"

"Don't count on it," Sophie said in a high-pitched voice. "Eden might not be allowed to come back here. They might think he's better off in a group home. Who could blame them?" She blew her nose and rushed off to the bathroom.

Mikey turned to Hannah, "Don't you think he'd be good at building models?"

"Oh yeah," said Hannah. "Amazing!"

Mikey blushed. "Don't be so sarcastic!"

Hannah wriggled her fingers in front of his face. "You will actually permit him to touch your train?"

Mikey's face was now a shining red. "Who was so mean about Gladly?" he cried. "It wasn't as though he hurt her or anything. You kept saying I was jealous. It was you who was the jealous one!"

Hannah laughed at his accusations. She pushed him back against the table and tickled him until he was squealing for mercy. "Edenitis! Edenitis!" she chanted.

CHAPTER SIXTEEN

By Sunday morning, no one was laughing. They went to a special church service for Eden. Most of the Sounds people were there, including those who went to church only for weddings and funerals. Mikey thought that from the way they looked, it was a kind of funeral, even though they were praying for Eden's safety.

Sergeant Duff had put it into words last night. "You realize," he said to Joe and Sophie, "that at this stage we are looking for a body."

The search was being scaled down. The dogs and their handlers had left, and some of the Sounds people were returning to work. Joe was one of a group of six who would go out again after the service. They were looking in different places now, at the bottom of cliffs and along rivers.

A lot of people cried in church. Mikey was one of them. He felt embarrassed. Not because his eyes were dripping, but because his nose was running, too, and he didn't have a tissue or handkerchief. He pulled down the sleeves of his sweatshirt and pretended he was scratching his face; then he tried to hide the wet patch.

After the service, a list of names was taken for small groups of searchers who would go out every day. Mikey knew that Joe would be in each group. He wouldn't stay home until Eden was found.

Mikey wanted to go with him that afternoon.

"He's strong," said Sophie. "He can keep up."

"No!" said Joe, giving Sophie a look.

Mikey thought, "He doesn't want me just in case they find a body."

Joe left with Mr. Godsiff and four other men in a four-wheel-drive vehicle. Sky stayed at the Godsiffs' house to play. Sophie drove Hannah and Mikey home, and as they got near the driveway, Mikey said, "Sophie, will you take me down to look at the eel trap?"

"We've got nothing better to do," Sophie said.

They were quiet for a long time. Far too long. The weight of the silence made Mikey's skin itch. He said, "I reckon he's alive."

"So do I," said Hannah. "I feel it in my bones."

Sophie straightened her arms against the steering wheel. "Joe says that Sergeant Duff really knows what he's talking about."

"I don't care," said Hannah. "Eden isn't dead."

"I didn't mean that," said Sophie. "I was thinking of the way Sergeant Duff kept coming back to those stories. Did you tell him everything, Hannah?"

"Most of it," said Hannah. "It's hard to remember everything."

"What was the episode the night before Eden left?" Sophie asked.

"Sergeant Duff asked me that three times. Nothing. We didn't have a story."

"Hannah was mad at Eden for riding Gladly," Mikey said.

"What about the night before?" Sophie asked.

Hannah thought. "I can't remember."

"Nothing again," said Mikey. "We were late getting back from Christchurch."

"Well then, before that," said Sophie. "On Monday night."

Hannah shook her head. "I don't know."

"I do," said Mikey. "It was pukifying. This giant rimu had been wounded by a chain saw, and it was dying."

"You weren't even listening!" said Hannah

"There's a difference between listening and hearing," he said.

"That was it," Hannah said to Sophie. "They got the water of life to save the rimu giant, and it gave them three wishes…"

"Stop the car!" Mikey cried. "This is where I get out."

Sophie put on the brakes, and they were all flung forward in their seat belts. She said, "Do you want us to come, too?"

Mikey guessed that he'd have to listen to the story again, spun out over the path along the riverbank. "No thanks. Wait for me. I won't be long."

There were two small silverbelly eels in the trap. He didn't have the sack with him. He wondered about carrying the eels in the trap back to the car, but the thought made him tired. He was getting sick of eeling.

He carefully lifted out one of the eels and felt it sliding through his hands like a slippery whip. He dropped it into the water, where it disappeared with a small splash. He let the other go in the same way, wiped his hands on the grass, and then returned to the road.

"You didn't get anything?" Hannah said.

"No." He got in the car.

"You smell like eel," she said.

"I left the trap up on the bank. I think I'll give it a rest for a while."

Sophie said, "Mikey, we've decided to go up the Titirangi Road."

"Why?"

"We're not sure why. Do you remember that place where we stopped to get some lichen last Sunday?"

"Not really. I didn't get out of the car."

"That's where the huge rimu is," Hannah said. "It's half-dead, got a big split in it. That's why we put it in the story. We could get right inside the wound. Eden was jumping in and out, and so was I. Then I saw a big weta this far from his face. I yelled at him to get out. You know what he did?"

"Picked it up in his hand?" said Mikey.

"How did you know that?"

"It was an awesomely difficult guess," Mikey said.

They drove up the steep, rocky road and into the somber, dark trees. "Haven't they searched here dozens of times?" Mikey asked.

"Yes, they have," said Sophie.

"Then why are we doing it again?"

Sophie replied. "I don't know, Mikey. It's just a feeling Hannah and I have. But we've had other feelings that haven't amounted to anything."

They stopped where they had parked last Sunday and helped each other up the steep bank. Last Sunday the bank had been dry. Now it was running with small trickles of water, and the moss on it oozed like wet sponges. On top, they were in beech forest. Walking was not easy.

The space between the black-trunked trees was filled with a net of broken branches and small saplings. Mikey was wearing canvas sneakers, which were already squishing with wetness.

"How far are we going?" he asked.

"Not far," said Hannah.

That answer always annoyed him. "How long is not far?"

"As long as a piece of string," Hannah called back.

They seemed to know the way. They climbed over fallen logs and brushed aside ferns, breathing fast with their haste. Everything was wet. Trees dripped, lichen oozed. Even on the steeper slopes, the undergrowth sank beneath their feet like a bog.

"Are you sure this is the right direction?" he asked.

"I think so," Sophie replied.

"What do you mean, you think so?" He was puffing. "You weren't away all that long."

"Over there!" pointed Hannah, and she took off in a new direction.

"Oh fantiddlytastic!" he muttered, borrowing Sky's word. "Next Sunday they'll have a church service for four missing people."

"It's the only rimu tree among the beech," said Hannah, "It's so big you can't miss it."

From a distance it looked more like a tall garden than a tree. It was so overgrown with green stuff—moss, lichen, ferns, clumps of orchids—Mikey couldn't see the wood of the trunk. Hannah was right. It was quite different from the surrounding beech trees.

Hannah started to run. She went leaping, crashing through the undergrowth and broken branches, falling, getting up again. From where Mikey was she looked like a frantic butterfly. She got to the tree, walked around it, and stopped.

Sophie and Mikey struggled to catch up.

Hannah looked at them and said quietly, "He's here."

Mikey got an awful, sick feeling, and his skin went cold. He wanted to stay where he was. Sophie hesitated, too. Then they both ran.

At the base of the big rimu, sticking out from the ferns, was a mud-stained sneaker and foot. As Sophie came close, Hannah took a couple of steps backward.

"Oh dear God!" said Sophie, and she parted the wet fern.

Eden was lying in the split of the tree, a dark hollow almost like a cave. His head was on his bag. He was breathing. The in and out of his chest made a fast, rasping sound. His eyes were closed. He was so covered with mud that he looked like some vegetable dug up from a wet garden.

"Eden! Oh Eden, darling boy!" Sophie cried.

She reached into the hollow and tried to lift him up. His eyelids fluttered, and he gave a shriek of pain.

"His leg!" said Hannah.

Above the foot that had been sticking out of the fern, his jeans were ripped almost to the thigh. Between his ankle and knee there was a bulge like an extra kneecap.

Sophie set him back gently. "Eden? Can you hear me, Eden?"

His eyelids fluttered again, and he made a grunting noise.

Sophie took off her jacket and put it over him. "He has a high fever," she said. "Eden? It's Sophie. You're going to be all right now, Eden."

His lips moved. Sophie put her head right into the hollow, close to his face. "I think he wants a drink. He's very dehydrated. Broken leg, pneumonia, I don't know what else. He'll have to go out on a stretcher. I'm going back to the car. I have to find a phone."

"An ambulance?" asked Mikey.

"No. The helicopter. It can be here in twenty minutes."

"What do you want us to do?" Mikey asked.

"Talk," said Sophie. "Keep talking to him. Hannah, you'd better come back to the car with me. There's a plastic bowl in the back. You can get him some of the water trickling by the road. Give it to him in little sips. Be very careful."

"That water'll have germs in it," said Mikey.

"We'll worry about that later. Mikey, don't try to move him, and don't leave him for a second."

They went off running. The crashing noise sounded like wild pigs in the undergrowth, and Mikey wondered what would happen if a mean old boar ambled along. Wild pigs ate newborn lambs. He leaned into the tree cave and was surprised to see that Eden had his eyes open. "You okay?" Mikey asked.

Eden nodded.

"They've gone for help. Guess what? You're going to get a helicopter ride. The kids at school will be jealous. They'll eat their own heads when they find out."

Eden watched him. In the dry mud mask of his face, his eyes gleamed like pale stones.

"We missed you," said Mikey. "Sophie had to give your share of the pizza to the hens." He stopped. Eden had closed his eyes again.

"They found Gladly all right. The Webbs brought her home. When you're better, you can help me build my railway. If you want to, of course."

Eden's breathing was loud and fast. Talk to him, Sophie had said. Okay, okay, he was talking.

"I got two eels today, but I threw them back. I thought you'd like to know that. And hey, Joe knows that pocketknife is yours. Mrs. Godsiff told Sophie. It's a fantabulous knife.

Did you know it has scissors?"

Eden didn't move.

"Hannah's going to be here soon with some water. You have enough to eat? Bread and stuff? Guess you ran out. Bread's pretty boring, anyway, although French toast is good. I'll make you some of that when we get home. Are you warm enough?"

It was useless asking questions. He'd run out of things to say. He heard a rustling sound in the undergrowth and looked for Hannah. She wasn't there. "It'll be a weka," he told himself. "Just a weka. Talk! Go on, talk!"

"Hey Eden, you know how you told me you used to smoke hundreds and hundreds of packs of cigarettes? I didn't think about that being a story like Hannah's stories. I got it wrong. As you might have guessed, stories aren't my thing. Sorry I got mad at you."

Eden opened his eyes again and looked at Mikey.

"How many packs did you really smoke?"

Eden's mouth moved but no sound came out. He lifted his right hand to show three fingers.

"Didn't it make you feel sick?" Mikey reached into the hollow and held the raised hand. It was hot, dry and scaly with mud. Eden tried to answer. His face flickered; then his eyes half-closed and his hand, still in Mikey's, fell sideways against the tree.

Mikey stayed there holding Eden's hand until Hannah came back. She was carrying a white plastic bowl of water, but Eden wouldn't wake up for a drink. She put her finger in the water and wet the inside of his mouth.

"He feels really hot," she said.

Mikey said, "How do you tell the difference between someone sleeping and someone unconscious?"

"I don't know." Hannah sat down, took off her right shoe and sock, and then put her shoe back on her bare foot. She poured some water over the sock and started wiping the mud off Eden's face.

Mikey said, "When he finds out you washed his face with your dirty sock, he's going to die—" He stopped, biting off the word.

Eden looked so bad he might die anyway.

The roar of the helicopter was sudden. It burst over their heads and faded, but not completely. They could hear its blades beating in the distance and later learned that it had landed in the nearby gravel pit. Sophie had waited down there to guide the two paramedics to the rimu tree.

The men checked Eden from head to toe. They looked in his eyes and mouth, felt his head, neck, shoulders, stomach, and took his blood pressure. They put a needle into his arm with a tube connected to a plastic bag. Then they strapped his leg into a plastic splint. All the time, they talked to him, telling him what they were doing, even though his eyes were closed and he wasn't answering.

They carried the stretcher out of the forest and down the road to the helicopter. As they slid Eden in behind the pilot's seat, Mikey glimpsed his pale, mud-smeared face and thought what a pity it was that he didn't know he was flying.

Chapter Seventeen

Sergeant Duff told them Eden had truly believed that they were going to send him away. "It had happened to him so often before. He was sure it would happen again. So he ran away to the magic forest."

"He knew it wasn't real!" said Hannah.

"Ah, maybe. But then that day when you went to Titirangi you showed him it was real. You showed him the tree. He climbed that tree to hide from one of the search parties. He thought they were the Doomroths. After they were gone, he had trouble getting down. That's when he slipped and broke his leg."

"You don't think he tried to fly like Drakmar?" Hannah said.

"No, he said he slipped. Nothing about flying. I'm sure he didn't try to live out all the details of the story. I got the impression he wasn't sure whether he was Drakmar or whether he was Eden searching for Raku and Drakmar.

You know how it is with make-believe. I look at my little girl playing. She's a pirate or a queen. She's also herself. And she doesn't know where the boundary is between herself and the role she is playing. Eden didn't know, either."

"Why did he take Gladly?" asked Hannah.

"He felt strongly that since Raku had Sassenach, Drakmar should also have a horse. He was taking Gladly to the magic forest."

"Then why did he abandon her?"

"He didn't. She ran away, and he had to continue on his own. He hid several times from Doomroths, he said. So much for our clever search dogs! By the second night, he reached the tree." Sergeant Duff looked at Hannah. "The most important part of the story was the bit that you forgot. In the last episode, the tree was healed from a chain saw cut, and it told Raku and Drakmar to come back for three wishes."

"That's right," said Hannah. "The three wishes were going to be in the next episode."

"Eden didn't know where to find Raku and Drakmar, but he knew they were coming back to the tree to get their wishes. All he had to do was wait by the tree for them." Sergeant Duff gave Hannah one of his huge smiles. "He was right. Raku did eventually come—and just in time, as all good stories go. Another day and there would have been an entirely different ending."

It was a two-and-a-half hour journey to

Blenheim and the hospital, but they visited him twice a week. So did almost every other family in the Sounds. The hospital room was always full of people, and he had enough fruit to feed an elephant.

"You should tell them you're a junk food freak," said Mikey, tossing a bag of chips on the bed.

"Both now," said Eden. "Junk food with fruit in between. Thanks, Mikey."

Hannah had brought in her felt pens so that they could draw more pictures on his cast. His leg was still in traction, hoisted high above the bed, and they had to be careful they didn't lean on it while they were scribbling messages. Hannah drew Gladly with a speech bubble coming out of her mouth and the words, "A broken leg is no excuse."

Joe said, "Your doctor says you are well and truly over the pneumonia. Another week and your leg comes out of traction. They'll put a lighter cast on it so you can start walking. Then you'll be getting new artwork, I guess."

"When can I go home?" Eden asked.

"They're not giving dates yet," said Sophie. "But it won't be long."

"It's so boring in here," he said.

"I wish I was you," Sky said, "Look at all the presents you got! Cards, grapes, toys. You even have your own TV!"

"I'll be glad to swap you," Eden said.

"Any day!" said Sky.

Sophie ruffled Sky's hair. "Big talk! You don't have a fraction of Eden's patience. You'd be shrieking boredom after two hours, not to mention two weeks. Eden, Hannah's not saying anything, so I'll have to tell you this. She's made something special for you—a beautiful book."

"Me and Mikey helped with the pictures," said Sky.

Hannah wrapped her arms around the book, feeling awkward. "It's nothing much."

"Nothing?" shrieked Sky. "It's fantiddly-tastic!"

"Come on, everyone," said Joe. "The Gerritsens are outside. We'll go and talk to them and let Hannah give Eden his book. Come on, Sky. You heard me."

They left the room, and Hannah put the book on the bed. "It really is nothing. Just the story. You see—um—I'm telling it to Sky. He couldn't wait for you to get out of the hospital. And we didn't want you to miss any of it, so I—so we—"

"Raku and Drakmar?" Eden picked up the book and opened it.

"I tried to do it in neat printing."

"Will you read it to me?"

"No. You read it to yourself."

He turned to the first page, putting his finger under the words.

"Afterward," said Hannah. "When you are bored."

He closed it and smiled at her. "Hannah, can I be your boyfriend?"

She was so surprised she didn't know what to say. She almost laughed but his face was serious.

"You got a boyfriend already?" he asked.

"No! Course not!" Then she said, "Eden, you're only ten."

"I'll be eleven soon." He frowned. "Okay, can I be your boyfriend when I'm thirteen?"

"By then I'll be sixteen," Hannah said. "I'll be away at boarding school, and you'll be rounding up sheep with Gladly." She shrugged. "Anyway, you can't be my boyfriend if you're my brother."

"Oh yeah," he said. He looked at the book. "Will you write me some more about Raku and Drakmar?"

"Yes. I promise."

"What happens when the story ends?"

Hannah laughed. "Oh, that's easy," she said. "We just begin a new one."